Silma Hill

Bloks Bergs
Verrichtung.

Silma Hill

Iain Maloney

First published 2015

Freight Books
49-53 Virginia Street
Glasgow, G1 1TS
www.freightbooks.co.uk

A CIP catalogue reference for this book is available from the British Library

ISBN 978-1-908754-93-6
eISBN 978-1-908754-94-3

Typeset by Freight in Plantin
Printed and bound by Bell and Bain, Glasgow

the publisher acknowledges investment from
Creative Scotland toward the publication of this book

FOR PATRICIA AND MICHAEL

EARTH

1

THE REVEREND E. S. BURNETT, MINISTER for the parish of Abdale, was composing his sermon when his daughter intruded. At her apologetic knock he paused, nib hovering over Romans 15:4: "For whatsoever things were written aforetime were written for our learning, that we through patience and comfort of the scriptures might have hope." He waited his customary ten seconds, pen dripping, before a granite, 'Come!' He rubbed the ink from his pale, soft hands, the only marks on them graft from the labour of his mind. His study was wood-panelled and book-lined, a lifetime of accumulated knowledge, theological texts, scientific treatise, drawers of correspondence. The fruits of man's explorations since the Fall there for him to harvest. Removing his glasses he ran his finger over the groove they had worn in the bridge of his nose. The ploughed furrows in his forehead, the widow's peak and curl in his once broad shoulders spoke of the hours he spent hunched over a thick book or a blank sheet.

Fiona's hands, pressed heavy against the door, were those of a woman much older than herself, barnacled with a near-decade of work. Sixteen and already care-worn, she approached the frontier of his citadel. There was no telling what reception she would receive, what choler had aggravated his temper. A storm may be gathering over his desk waiting for a conductor on which to break. The Lord was strong and wrathful. Reverend Burnett, his representative.

'Begging your pardon, sir,' she said. 'Old Man... I mean

Mister Sangster is at the kitchen door. He says he has found something. Something in which you may have an interest.' He considered her with a stern eye, weighing her with the experienced consideration of a judger of men. Her voice was too harsh, the local accent too strong, the vowels too parochial. Steps needed to be taken. The sons of important men would never marry a wench with a mouth so common. The daughter of a respected minister and future member of the Historical Antiquities Society should be beyond reproach.

Burnett stood slowly, stretching his limbs out from the seat, reaching for his hat where it rested on the bust of Calvin. A discovery by Sangster would shift the face of his week but there was no need to rush. Let the old fool wait. Burnett was a man immersed in complex spiritual matters, a man wrestling with the nature of the Lord, the glory of His Creation, saving the damned souls of Abdale. The parishioners couldn't expect him to respond to every trivial request with haste. Each man had his place in the Lord's grand scheme, and Sangster's was at the kitchen door, hat in hand. He waved Fiona away. She retreated to the pantry, alone in the darkness amongst the preserves and grains, the scratching of mice and the musk of old wood. Burnett's existence moved between the twin poles of his study and the kirk, and while he was secluded she had the manse to herself. When he walked abroad in her world, she tried to become a ghost, unseen, forgotten. It was safer that way.

As he passed through his house he searched for anything out of place. The manse gave him some satisfaction. High ceilings, solid walls, uncluttered, austere, every inch under his control. A man's home reflected his soul. Upon entering a home of squalor, of fetid stench and decay, of broken furniture and bestrewn floors, he knew there lived the damned. Parishioners concerned for the repose of their eternal soul need only glance around their abodes for an answer. Evidence abounded.

Twenty years before, arriving in Abdale a freshly made minister with a young wife, he had found the manse an abomination. The minister who preceded him, Cullen, was a simpleton, delighting in art and fancy. The manse reflected his tastes. Watercolours, many of them by Cullen himself, offended the walls. Flowers, ornaments, trinkets of such irrelevance that Burnett had wondered if Cullen had been a serious man in any way. Everything that could be burned was burned, the rest dumped. He had given orders. His wife had obeyed.

The manse had remained the same ever since. Fiona maintained it tolerably well. Not with the same surety and efficiency as Moira, may she rest in peace with the Lord, but these things were sent to test mankind. If Burnett could not educate his own child and order his own residence, he had no business educating and ordering his parishioners.

Sangster was waiting at the kitchen door, fingers filthy, back curled. The Sangsters were farmers, but had a hand in much that went on in the village, including the digging and selling of peat. It was in this capacity that the old man's existence proved valuable for Burnett. Peat bogs were excellent sites of discovery, preserving the treasures of history until ripe for reclamation. Over the years Sangster's clumsy fingers had unearthed Roman coins, shards of pottery, even a claymore. Finds he dutifully handed over to Burnett, the authority on such things.

Antiquities were Burnett's passion. He read widely on the subject, his shelves heaving with learned texts. He corresponded with the leading experts of the day, men of knowledge at the universities, the Royal Society and the Historical Antiquaries Society, the missives carefully filed. His finds methodically written up and submitted, copies sent to the relevant authorities. To date all he had received were watery letters thanking him for his contribution, curt notes, displaying vague sentiments. He had been to lectures at the Society, heard papers read, asked apposite questions, engaged in debates, but the doors to its inner sanctum remained sealed. They took him for a country minister. Typical of the city breed, he thought.

Self-absorbed, unable to see work of real clarity and insight when it was right in front of them. Too much claret. Too many feasts. One day he would produce work of such high and clear learning they would have no recourse but to make room at their table.

He strode through the kitchen to where Sangster was waiting. 'Sangster.'

'Good morning, Mister Burnett.'

'You have found something?' He was carrying it wrapped in a fraying grey blanket, delicately held in both hands. It was long, between four and five feet.

Sangster was a man of few words. Brevity was a holy virtue, even in a man as rough as him. Sangster laid the package on the ground and unwrapped it. Inside was a wooden object, a rough statue of human form carved from a single piece of dark wood. Long and thin, with grooves suggesting limbs, an unnaturally extended, narrow neck and an egg-shaped head, a flat slash for a mouth. It had absorbed some damage, chips serrated its edges, and the legs ended at the ankles, the feet long gone. It was female. Full breasts and an over-emphasised reproductive area. The eyes demanded attention. Two round brass pins raised from the head, the coloured metal fierce against the wood. The dirt that clung to the body had seemingly avoided the eyes, ringed them like exhaustion. They shone as though recently polished, a fervent light.

He crouched down beside Sangster. It was a false idol of some sort. Heathen. Before the light of Christianity came to the area it had been under the sway of a number of different barbarian sets. Celts, Romans, Norsemen. Burnett couldn't immediately tell which but he could conclude one thing: great care had been taken over its creation.

The eyes gave off an uncanny power. The power of graven images. Therein lies the appeal of false idols, why they have power over the imagination of weaker men. It was a mere object, carved by a man. To anyone with any intelligence the trickery was clear.

'Where did you find it?'

'North corner of the bog, Mister Burnett.'

The bog was on the far side of Silma Hill, which rose up behind the manse. Sangsters' beasts roamed the nearside. On the top of the hill stood a small copse and the remains of a stone circle. 'I'm going to examine it now, but I shall be down later today to sketch the site.' Burnett wrapped it carefully and carried it protectively inside.

2

AFTER THE CLICK OF HIS STUDY door, Fiona counted to one hundred before vacating the pantry. He'd tracked muddy footprints through the house, a trail like some bog creature had stalked by. With bucket and brush she set to scrubbing the boards for the second time that day.

So, Old Man Sangster had found something. Well, perhaps it would keep her father deskbound until Sunday, with that stout door firmly closed. If she were truly blessed, it would be so weighty a find as to take him to Edinburgh visiting those stuffed shirts whose arses he kissed. A week without muddy footprints, preparing three square meals, without hiding in the pantry. The brush flew over the wood, the dirt mixing with the water, seeping into the rags she used to dry and polish. A week of rising when she liked, of eating what she liked. Eilidh and Mary could come over for tea, sit out in the garden chattering and laughing like normal girls. She could see Murdoch without fear of discovery. As she cleaned she prayed that old Sangster had found something that would change everything, even for a day or two.

The floor clean again, she returned to the kitchen and finished packing the picnic. A practised look across the room then she got her mirror out. The bonnet she wore while cleaning could be discarded and she brushed some life back into her blonde hair. If only she could do something about the skin on her hands, but short of gloves nothing could hide the ruin done by her duties. What chance her father buying her anything as lavish as a pair of gloves? Her birthday had flown by barely acknowledged but for a copy of John Knox's *The First Blast of the Trumpet Against the Monstrous Regiment of Women,* and prayers by the graveside.

Birthdays for Fiona were days of mourning, when her and Burnett were united in grief. Her mother had died in childbirth. Fiona's entry into God's ledger had been her mother's exit, their lives crossing for a few precious seconds. Before Fiona had caught her breath, before the natal cry had burst from her chest, her mother's soul was escaping her weak flesh and returning to the Lord. Her eyes had never looked on her mother's face. Her parents had been married but a short term. Moira had left little mark on the world besides Fiona's existence. Her clothes long gone, Burnett returned them to her family then broke contact after the funeral. He could bear no reminder of his loss. Fiona, already denied a mother, was then denied her remembrance, save prayers and flowers at her grave. But nature will conspire to fill emptiness, and so during lonely childhood nights she invented an image based partly on her own features and partly on pictures of the Virgin mother. She spoke to this invisible parent, directing prayers to her in Heaven, asking her advice, her help. As she grew older these conversations became less frequent, but in times of great strain, in the cold hours of a sleepless night, she sometimes invoked this fictional mother to speak words of comfort, to offer advice, to say everything would be all right, in the end. She felt her mother was there, always, watching over her. Mrs Galbraith, the former housekeeper, had told her stories of Moira's kindness, her popularity in the village, her beauty. When Fiona turned seven, Mrs Galbraith was let go. Three years later she too died. Since then it had been Fiona and her father alone, together.

Tying her shawl around the lunch, she placed it into her shopping basket and slipped quietly out through the kitchen door. Every day at about this time she ran errands in the village, so her absence from the manse would be expected. Not that he would notice, not now he had some new hobby-horse to fixate on.

She wasn't going into the village.

Fiona had a rendezvous. Old Man Sangster's grandson, Murdoch, was minding the beasts on the hill.

At the end of the garden she passed through the gap in the laurel hedge and into the field. It was about the right time of year for morel mushrooms and that was her excuse should he happen to demand an explanation later. She kept an eye out for some just in case.

Silma Hill was one of the highest points in the area. Abdale sat on the northern bank of a sea loch, a wrinkle in an ancient coastline, far enough inland that crops grown in the fertile soil were spared the salt of the sea. In days long gone the loch had been a shelter for boats during storms, and a base for Viking raids, the river connecting it with the ocean being deep and wide enough for safe passage. These days few vessels broached the dark waters save local fishermen and the cable ferry Old McBain piloted whenever a villager had business to the south. Once a busy town on the road north, a new military road now skirted the far side of the loch through Glentrow. There were no rebellions against the crown here, no Jacobites this far south. Glentrow got the benefit of troop movements and Abdale lay forgotten, abandoned in a kink of the Atlantic coast.

Fiona arrived first. Murdoch would meander casually up the far side of the field. The climb made her hot and she took a moment to wipe her face, calm her breath, arranging herself precisely so when Murdoch arrived she'd be a portrait come to life.

The summit of the hill had, in hazy history, been a site for some kind of ritual. A circle of sparkling granite stones once stood proud, now all but three of them lay fallen, some broken, one or two almost swallowed by the hill, surrounded by a copse of trees. In the shade, Fiona used one prone monolith as a table, and spread out the lunch things, the bread, eggs, cheese, leftovers from last night's dinner cunningly presented to look freshly prepared. She could hear him approach, cursing as he stumbled over some root or rabbit hole.

Murdoch was tall and thin. In one hand he held the stripped branch he used as a walking stick, an affectation she found adorable. In the other, a rag for wiping sweat. He looked like he might snap in a cruel wind but underneath his permanently dishevelled farm clothes he was wiry and strong.

'Morning lass,' he said.

'It's hardly morning anymore.'

He sat on the rock table, rested his stick against the edge. It rolled, landing in the brush with a soft pat, its burnished white flesh bright against the grass and scrub.

'The day hasn't started properly until I've seen you.'

'Away with you,' she laughed. 'Are you hungry?'

He ate fast, ravenous. All morning he'd been repairing the stone dyke, moving rocks, balancing, supporting. It was hard going, bent over, lifting, testing, over and again. At least it wasn't digging. At the foot of Silma Hill, on the far side from the manse, lay the peat bog. His grandfather was digging and cutting peat bricks to sell as fuel. Murdoch hated the peat, the smell, the squelch.

'Slow down, will you? You look like you haven't eaten in a fortnight.'

He slackened his pace for a moment then resumed his normal speed. She nibbled at a piece of cheese, not particularly hungry.

'I saw the old man over your way,' Murdoch said through a mouthful of bread. 'Anything interesting?'

'He found something in the bog.'

'And handed it over to your old man?'

'Aye.'

Murdoch shook his head. His father was forever on at his grandfather to stop handing over his finds to Burnett. They were probably worth something, maybe more than something. Giving them over was madness. Bits of broken pottery were all right but that claymore had been several steps too far. There'd be another fight at home that night.

'Well, if it keeps him busy,' she said, 'then I've got more time to spend with you.'

'That's true,' he said, swallowing. It looked like he was done, so Fiona wrapped what remained and returned it to her basket. He lifted his arm and she rested in against his shoulder.

Between swaying branches she looked out over Abdale, smoke rising from chimneys, folk chatting by the cross, the kirk steeple, the peak of Ben Morvyn, fields of new growth. 'Are you minding the beasts again tomorrow?' They had a number of assignation sites, but this was by far the easiest, being so close to the manse yet secluded.

'I think so,' he said. 'Or I'll be digging peat.' She hoped not. Digging meant he'd be able to make it up the hill for lunch, but he'd be covered in dirt and stink. Murdoch lay back on the rock, hands behind his head, hat down over his eyes. He's going to sleep? She couldn't be too angry. He looked peaceful lying there, her man. She wanted nothing more than to marry him, to bring him lunch every day and lie down next to him at night. Her father would never allow it. Not a farmer's son, and certainly not a Sangster. She wasn't sure he'd allow her to get married at all. He'd keep her as his slave until she was a spinster and Murdoch had married one of the other girls. If he did let her marry, there was little hope he'd let her choose.

She heard a shout, and looked down towards the manse, hidden by the green canopy. Nobody. The shout came again. She ran to the other side, peered through the branches down to the peat bog. At the far end she could see two figures, one lying down, the other bent over the first. She called Murdoch.

'It's my Da,' he said. 'And my Granda.'

'What are they doing?'

'Doesn't look good. I'd better go down.'

'I'll return home.'

'Right, love. Thanks for the food.' He pushed through the branches and ran down the hill. She watched for a moment, wondering what had happened and then, pausing only to grab her basket, rushed back to the manse.

3

MURDOCH RAN DOWN SILMA HILL, SWERVING rabbit holes, his boots thumping the ground like a heartbeat. He leapt a pool, landed soft and shifted direction in one swift movement, taking off along the path through the uneven damp ground of the bog. His father, Dougie, saw Murdoch and beckoned. The old man was on his back, legs hanging over the peat face. 'Hurry up, boy,' Dougie called. 'Give me some help.'

'What happened?' he asked, getting hold of his grandfather's legs, pulling him back onto more solid land, laid him out. He was painted in peat.

'He was slow coming back with the peat so I came to see the problem. Found him pitched over in there. Where were you?'

'With the beasts.'

'I didn't see you on the way by.'

'No?' Murdoch didn't look up. The road from their farm to the bog ran along the burn between the manse and Silma Hill. From there his father would have had a clear view of the beasts in the field, unattended by Murdoch. Dougie had cleared the peat from the old man's face but it was too late. He was dead. Silent, hats off in respect, each said a prayer for his soul. The wind picked up for a moment, rolling down off Silma Hill, rippling the grass around them.

'Must have been his heart.'

'Aye,' said Murdoch. 'He made a good age.'

'Aye. Must've been down a while.'

'How?'

'He hasn't cut more than a handful of bricks.'

'Oh,' said Murdoch, 'no, he found something, took it over to the manse.' He remembered too late who told him.

'See him, did you?'

'Eh, aye. From the field.' Would he mind? Minister's daughter? Burnett's daughter?

'Help me get him on the barrow,' his father said. 'We'll get him home.'

'Do you want me to go tell Burnett?'

'No, I'll do it. I'm the son after all. It'll be your turn to arrange a funeral one day. No point rushing it. You can go and wake up Jimmy Ross, let him know.'

Jimmy Ross was the nightwatchman, the representative of the law in Abdale. He had little power himself but as the subordinate of Sheriff Dawkins, based in Glentrow, anything like a birth or a death had to be reported to him. There had been no crime of any note in Abdale for years and Jimmy didn't bother patrolling anymore. They were far from any major roads so passing travellers, vagabonds and highway men were rarer than unicorns. Once there had been a constable in addition to a nightwatchman, and a tollbooth built for their use, but with the new road and the lack of traffic, the tollbooth stood empty and a constable's wage considered a waste. Only Jimmy Ross remained, the eyes of the law in Abdale, paid by the Sheriff's office in Glentrow.

They cleared the peat barrow and got him up on it, pushed him home through the streets of the village. People came out to see and, when they learned of the tragedy, to pay their respects, to ask God to care for his soul and thank Him that it wasn't their family that suffered this time. All said he'd reached a good age, had a long life, his heart was it? Mercifully fast that way, the Lord forgive me.

Murdoch went round to Angus Grant, the carpenter, for a coffin and then on to Ross. Dougie went to see Burnett.

Murdoch's mother, Shona, and his sister, Eilidh, prepared the body. Shona got on with the job, stripping the corpse of its encrusted clothes. Both her own parents were dead and this task had been her responsibility then. Sleeves rolled up over strong arms and hair tied back, experience severed her emotions from her actions. It had to be done. 'Not like that, Eilidh, like this.' Eilidh was dabbing tenderly when scrubbing was needed, tears streaking her thin, pale face. She'd been close to her grandfather and expected every touch to wake him. She sobbed throughout, more hindrance than help. But she had to learn.

Old Mrs Sangster, plump and wrinkled, sprouting like a forgotten potato, took the news stoically, sat in her chair and watched as they redressed him, brushed the few wisps of remaining white hair into place. 'When he was a young lad,' she said as they worked, 'he was fascinated with the Vikings that used to raid these lands. He found an arrow head down by the loch and that was him, off on daydreams of warriors and whatnot for years. Probably wasn't even anything to do with Norsemen, that arrow head, but he swore it was.'

Eilidh liked to hear stories of her grandparents' youth, particularly her grandfather. In old age – the only age she'd known him – he was quiet, reticent to the point of rudeness, allowing his wife to speak on his behalf. To think of him as a young man Murdoch's age, or as a boy, running around the loch playing war games with arrow heads allowed her to step into a world she'd never known, one where the silent old man who had sat uncomplaining as the child Eilidh clambered over him, had a spark, had vitality, something her grandmother had seen and liked.

'He always said he wanted to be buried in the Viking manner. After death their body and possessions were placed on a ship. The wife counted as a possession. The ship was pushed out onto the water. Then they would fire blazing arrows onto it, and the whole thing would burn to ashes, then sink. That is how he wanted to go. I told him no thank you very much. He is not taking me with him, not on a burning ship. Still, it would be a sight out there in the loch. Big Viking ship in flames. A famous way to go.' She relished the old tales, the ancient myths of the area. From her childhood she'd collected these stories, embellishing them in the retelling, elaborating, explaining, and using them to weave a tapestry of legend around Abdale.

'I think the Minister would have something to say about heathen burials,' said Shona.

Eilidh saw a flash like a shooting star across her grandmother's face and knew she was imagining the scene. She was perfectly capable of demanding a Viking burial for her husband purely to cause a fight with Burnett.

Like a draught down the back of Mrs Sangster's neck, chill realisation seeped into her blood. She gasped.

'What is it, Gran?'

'Quick, quick Eilidh, the mirrors, the water, anything reflective. You've got to cover them.' She pulled herself painfully out of her seat and threw her shawl over the mirror that rested on the mantelpiece. 'The others, all the mirrors in the house, cover them.'

'Oh, Mother,' said Shona. 'These superstitions.' But they obeyed.

'What's wrong with the mirrors, Gran?' asked Eilidh.

'His soul could get trapped,' she said. 'And then he would never get to Heaven. Hopefully we weren't too late. We will have to listen for thunder. That's the sign he has made it.'

4

BURNETT BEGAN BY SKETCHING THE STATUE. This approach had several benefits. If the object was particularly delicate he could work from the drawings rather than continually handling the piece. Furthermore, the attention required in drafting highlighted interesting details he may otherwise have missed. Slight chinks in a claymore blade, mementos of combat, or aspects of design on pots he had dismissed as age. Sat at his desk, the surface smothered in pencil and charcoal pictures, he entered a state he likened to the deep meditations of the great church thinkers, Luther, Calvin, Knox, even Aquinas and Augustine. By studying the progress of man from the Garden to this pinnacle of learning nearly eighteen hundred years after the birth of Christ, Burnett was exploring the grandeur of the Lord. Providence and science were two sides of the same coin. The pulpit was for teaching, the mind for worshipping. Any peasant could rest on a pew, say his prayers at night and remain idle on the Sabbath, but it took a person of great spiritual and intellectual gifts to pick apart Creation itself.

A clamour, like a sinner trying to escape through the gates of Hell, broke his concentration. Twice in one day. He began counting to ten, but as he reached six the door opened. He stood, and stepped towards the sideboard against which his birch rod leaned.

'Please, sir,' Fiona said. 'Excuse my interruption, but Mister Sangster is at the door.'

'Again? What does he want that's so important? Has he

found another piece?' A pair was too much to hope for.

'No, sir,' she said. 'Not that Mister Sangster. His son.'

'His son? The middle Sangster? What does he want?'

'It's the elder Sangster, sir—'

'What? They're both here?'

'No, sir—'

'Speak clearly, girl.'

'Sir, please. Mister Sangster is here. The middle Sangster. His father, the elder Sangster. He's dead.'

'What?' He left the study and turned towards the kitchen.

'No, sir. He's at the front door.'

A Sangster at the front door? He stopped, shook his head. 'Dead?'

'Yes, sir.'

'But he was just here.' Of course, the front door. This was business. Sangster Junior, Wee Sangster as he had been when Burnett first came to the parish, was here to see about his father's passage into the next world. He retrieved his hat from Calvin, straightened his clothes and opened the door. 'Mister Sangster,' he said, 'my daughter tells me the good Lord has gathered your father unto him.'

'Yes, Minister. I have come to make the necessary arrangements.'

'Of course. Please, come with me.' Resting a hand on Sangster's shoulder he steered him towards the kirk. The man seemed strong. That was good. Emotion made death odious. 'It must have been very sudden,' he said, leading Sangster through the kirk and into his office. 'I saw him only a few hours ago.'

'Yes, Minister. His heart, I suspect.'

'A quick death. The Lord is merciful. One moment with us, the next with Him.'

'He rose this morning, same as any other day.'

'The plan is only revealed to us afterwards. We must work as if we will see all our schemes to fruition, be it work of the body or of the mind, yet we must live with devotion in our hearts. Any moment may be our last. Death beds are denied many in these times. We never know when we will be standing before His door.'

'I believe,' said Sangster, 'my father stood before your door this morning.'

'That is correct,' he said, taking a seat behind his large mahogany desk, gesturing for Sangster to sit. 'He found a wooden statue.'

'An interesting find?'

'It's too early to tell,' said Burnett. 'Possibly a pagan relic, more probably a child's doll or some such frivolity. Now, shall we deal with these difficult but necessary details?'

Back in the house Fiona fretted from room to room, fiddling with flower arrangements, dusting already dust-free shelves. She wanted to rush over to Murdoch, but that was impossible. Besides, she was more than a touch fearful of being in their house. The old man, may the Lord have mercy on him, would be there, laid out in his box. Being the Minister's daughter she had seen more funerals, more grieving families than most but she had never become comfortable with the presence of death, to be at ease amongst ghosts other than her mother. Funerals were where the two worlds met, the living and the dead in the same place, communing, coming together for the passage of one from this world to that. Fiona couldn't help but put herself in the place of the widows and widowers, the children of parents gone, the parents of children taken. She had never made it through a funeral without sobbing.

She prayed silently, asked her mother to take care of Mr Sangster. She apologised to Mr Sangster's ghost for her selfishness, for enjoying a picnic while he was dying in the bog below. She asked for their forgiveness. She knew her mother heard.

Although dinner was hours away, she got the potatoes out and began preparing them. Something to do, to be moving.

What had her mother's funeral been like? Who had been there? Many times she had imagined it, her father standing at the head of the grave, officiating. Perhaps he showed emotion that day. Perhaps his voice caught on a word, perhaps he had to take a second try at a sentence. There must have been some love between them. There must have been, even if it died then. Had he been happy before her death, before Fiona's birth? The one came so hard upon the other. He was not one to question the Lord's plan, but perhaps he questioned this. If not for Fiona's birth, her mother would still be alive.

A sharp pain, white behind her eyes. The knife had gone clean through the tip of her thumb. She wrapped her apron tight around it, flinched at the material touch. The potatoes were red, blood over and under them, like after a slaughter. She breathed. Counted. Breathed. The pain faded from white, turned to dull agony. She leaned against the wall. Inside, where her skull met her neck, the whirling sensation died down, eased like a slowing wheel. She unwrapped the apron and saw it wasn't as bad as she feared, a flap of skin clung on. Flinching, she rinsed it, wrapped it again.

She could go over. Of course she could. Murdoch's sister, Eilidh, was her friend. It would be odd if she didn't go over to pay her respects. She just had to be careful. She was going as the minister's daughter, as Eilidh's friend. She sorted herself out, changed into her mourning clothes and set out for the Sangsters' farm. From the window of the kirk, Reverend Burnett watched her go.

5

EILIDH EXCUSED HERSELF AND WENT OUT into the warm spring sunshine. She needed respite from the presence of her grandfather stretched out awaiting his coffin. It was strange that the world was going on as normal, that the sun hadn't dipped in respect. The birds sang on, a rabbit darted across the lane oblivious to grief, and the MacFarlane's dog barked its usual round. She wiped her eyes and was about to check on the drying washing, flickering in the breeze, when she saw Fiona coming down the road. She ran to meet her. It was unseemly for the recently bereaved to be seen running, but Eilidh didn't care. Emotion had her wound up tight like a spinning top ready to go.

'Oh, Eilidh,' said Fiona, 'your father is over at the kirk now, he told me about your grandfather. I came to offer my deepest condolences.'

'Thank you, dear Fiona.' They hugged and Eilidh's tears dampened Fiona's neck. Eilidh glanced back at the house. 'Murdoch isn't here. He's seeing Angus about a box.'

'Let's go in,' Fiona said. 'I want to pay my respects to your mother and your grandmother.'

In the kitchen the shutters were closed and the women had changed into black. The difference in light, the sharp contrast in mood from outside caused Fiona to blink, to cough as if the air were composed of different elements. It took her a moment to realise that the old man lay on the stone floor. She stepped back, shocked, fought to regain control. She had expected to see a coffin, she had hoped there would be a lid on it. Him lying there like he'd had a slip. She coughed again, forgetfully clasping her hands together, squeezing pain from her thumb. Under the bandage she could feel it seeping still. 'Missus Sangster, I am so sorry for your loss.'

'Thank you, Fiona, come in and join us for some tea.' Fiona fixed her eyes on Shona and Eilidh, anywhere but the unnaturally still face of the man she had spoken to hours before. The three of them sat around the table and Shona poured out their cups.

'Where is Missus Sangster?' Fiona said.

'She's sleeping,' said Shona, with a roll of her eyes.

The Sangster home was a warren of rooms, nooks and chaos. Originally a two room cottage, as the family grew so too the house, branching out in several directions, a bedroom here, a bigger larder there, a patchwork of building materials. Fiona remembered being a small child and visiting with Mrs Galbraith when she came to buy eggs and milk, playing with Eilidh, running and hiding in this maze of a home. In all the years since, it had never lost its charm. Fiona often considered that if she married Murdoch, she would live with these women every day, wake and walk through these odd rooms and never think about leaving. To be a part of this household, the fun, the fights, the on-going drama of life as a Sangster. Silence settled like snow.

She searched for something to say, something to add. That was the problem – after the initial acknowledgment of the situation, what did you do? She looked around for a topic but her eyes fell each time on the corpse. Shona came to the rescue. 'She was saying earlier that he would have wanted a Viking burial.'

'A Viking burial?'

'Apparently they put you in a boat and set fire to it. Do you think your father would let something like that happen?'

'I don't see why not,' she said. 'Although I don't think you would get him wearing one of those helmets with the horns.' The three of them laughed at the image and Shona topped up the tea.

'Are you the cause of hilarity in this house of mourning, Miss Burnett?'

They turned to see old Mrs Sangster in the doorway. Fiona leapt to her feet and bowed low. 'Missus Sangster, I am here to offer my sincerest…'

'And we thank you for it. Shona, where's my drink?'

Shona handed over a cup of ale. Mrs Sangster would touch nothing else, and certainly not tea. Beer had been good enough for folk for generations, so it was good enough for her now. She had no taste for foreign muck. She settled into her chair like a monarch. Her body may have weakened with age but her will was undiminished. 'And who has been to pay respects?'

Fiona sat again, trying to keep the tea kettle between her and the body.

'The MacFarlanes and the Grants came by,' said Eilidh. 'Jimmy Ross as well.'

'Interfering as usual,' said Mrs Sangster. 'Some nightwatchman, him, asleep all night, awake all day.'

'He's got nothing to do,' said Shona.

'Probably hoping it was a murder so as he could investigate. Anyone else?'

'The Dalziels.'

The Dalziels? One Dalziel in particular, I would wager.' She gave Eilidh a lascivious wink.

'Aye, Malcolm came by. He's up at the kirk helping Old Hughie.'

'Helping? Hughie hasn't done a day's work in his life. He'll be sitting, legs hanging in the hole, pipe puffing away.' Old Mrs Sangster seemed to Fiona to be unaffected by the presence of her husband on the floor, carrying on as if this were any other day. She must be moved, surely the passing of her spouse broke her heart. An image of herself as an old woman, Murdoch carted home on the barrow, passed over her. A sob broke up her throat like a dove in her heart trying to escape. The grief would crack her in two, yet the old woman was joking. She thought of her mother. Her father. There must be grief. Surely.

'Here,' said the old woman. 'His eyes.' They looked at the body. Under the coins his eyes were still open.

'Aye,' said Shona. 'We couldn't get them closed.'

'Well see you get them shut before he goes in the ground. Can't meet his maker looking like he's sat on a hedgehog. And we can't take him out the house like that. If his eyes are open he'll see the route from the house to the grave and try to come back. Spirits don't want to leave their homes and will do anything to return. You have to close their eyes and take them out feet first so they don't know the way. And their eyes must be closed because if he looks at you death sees you through his eyes and you're next.'

Eilidh shivered, glanced around the room. Shona tried again to close the eyes but they were frozen open, an expression of shock. Fiona had to force herself to look away from those dark holes, their horrified expression. A noise outside, the door opened and Murdoch stood framed. He was surprised to see her but kept his composure. Behind him Angus Grant, the carpenter, and Malcolm Dalziel. They took the coffin into the kitchen and carefully lifted the old man into it. Shona replaced the coins over his eyes. Eilidh darted over to Malcolm, buried her face in his chest. Malcolm had the decency to look embarrassed. Fiona watched them, glanced at Murdoch's strong chest and long arms. The image of him on the barrow instead of his grandfather rose up before her again and she had to hang onto the seat to stop herself from copying Eilidh.

'Angus, Malcolm, tea?' said Shona.

'Thanking you,' said Angus.

'Not for me, Missus Sangster,' said Malcolm. 'I had better go and help Old Hughie.

'I'll go with him,' said Murdoch, 'see if Da needs a hand.'

'Well,' said Shona, 'you two gentlemen can escort Fiona home. I'm sure she doesn't want to spend the afternoon in a mourning house.'

'Oh no, Missus Sangster,' Fiona said. 'I'm happy to stay and help with anything you may need.'

'No, Fiona, there's not space enough for four of us in here now. Thank you for coming by.'

6

THE MANSE AND THE SANGSTERS' FARM marked the opposing limits of the village, east and west respectively. The occasional visitor arriving in Abdale by ferry would notice the kirk first, its grim spire lofty over all else manmade. To its right stood the manse, a solid granite box. Behind the village rose Silma Hill, crowned by the copse and stones. To reach the manse, Fiona, Murdoch and Malcolm would need to pass the kirk. She had no wish to be seen by her father with these two so she turned down the burn road and came at her home from behind. It was just as well she took the precaution because when Murdoch and Malcolm arrived at the kirk, business had been concluded and Mr Sangster had already left. The Minister was on his way back to his study. Burnett saw the pair approach and waited for them to reach him.

'Afternoon, Minister,' they both said, raising their caps.

'Afternoon,' he replied. 'Malcolm, you are here to help Old Hughie? He is by the plot.'

'Yes, sir.' Murdoch eyed his fast retreating back. Alone, together with Burnett. Fiona's father. An image of himself and Fiona on top of Silma Hill, her in his arms, their lips hotly meeting, his britches tightening at the touch of her body. Sweat creeped his back. His arms seemed suddenly superfluous, his hands fidgeted like they were possessed. He shoved them into his pockets. 'I seem to have missed my father,' he said. 'I had best be off to find him.'

'One moment,' Burnett said. 'I have need of a small favour.'

'Of course, Minister. How can I help you?'

'Your grandfather, God rest his soul, found something this morning which he turned over to me.'

'Aye, sir.'

'You knew?'

Twice he had done that. The muscles across his shoulders were tight, tense. 'I was in the top field this morning, sir, minding the beasts. I saw him go to your kitchen door.'

'Well, he was going to show me the find site later today, a very important detail in the scientific analysis of finds such as this. But now, of course, as the Lord in his infinite wisdom has taken him from us—'

'He was digging in the north east edge of the bog, sir,' said Murdoch, rolling a shoulder, easing the muscle.

'Ah, you know the spot? Excellent. Show me exactly where.' Murdoch nodded, took a step. 'A moment,' Burnett said. 'I must gather my implements.'

Murdoch waited on the grass outside, the urge to run tickling up his legs. A small tapping sound caught his attention: Fiona at the window. Murdoch gave her two thumbs up, mimed digging and pointed at the bog. She gave a quick look around her then blew him a kiss. He pretended to catch it. At that moment Burnett reappeared at the door, sketchbook in hand, long boots on. Murdoch froze, his hand raised, fist lightly formed around Fiona's kiss. She was gone from the window.

'What have you got there?'

'A butterfly, Minister.'

'A butterfly? This early in the year?'

'Eh, aye, sir. I used to collect them when I was wee.'

'Lepidoptery? A noble science. Let us examine the specimen.'

Slowly, he opened his hand. Empty. Burnett examined his face.

'Must have escaped, sir. While we were talking.'

Idiot boy. They all were around here. Good for manual

labour and the Lord's injunction to multiply, but that was their limit. Thank the Lord Fiona had never shown an interest in any of them. Burnett set off as though propelled, leading Murdoch through the gap in the hedge. Murdoch looked up at the summit of Silma Hill, at the thickness of the treeline. The beasts on the far side would remain unattended for a day or two and the peat would go uncut for longer. There had been more than enough work for three. Would two cope? He glanced back at the manse, saw a flicker of curtain. The seasons would roll round and one day he would take over the farm. From three to two, then to one. For the first time Murdoch seriously considered a future with children. A son would be a blessing then. 'What are you waiting for?' Burnett called. He looked again at the manse, at Silma Hill, then jogged to catch up, directed Burnett to the spot.

'He was definitely digging here?'

'Aye, sir. As you see he had only done a wee bit.'

That made things easier for Burnett. The few bricks Sangster had cut out must have been on top of the idol. He looked for the exact spot, the straight slashes of the spade, freshly made. Nothing. He could see the marks of older work, the edges collapsed, broken up and rough. 'It cannot have been here,' he said. 'There are no scars.'

Murdoch pointed at the marks. 'There, sir.'

'They are old, boy.'

'They are from this morning, sir.'

'Really?' he said. 'Then perhaps you can explain why they are not fresh and sharp?' He took up the spade, cut a section. 'That is new. Now compare it to those. I suppose you have a scientific explanation for that?'

'Aye, sir.' The chirp of insects and the low of the beasts. Murdoch regarded the condescending expression. This man, grandfather to his son? 'That one looks newer because it hasn't had a body lying on top of it.'

'Thank you, that will be all.'

7

OVER THE REST OF THE DAY people stopped by to pay their respects. After dinner Eilidh sought the refuge of her bed. She said a prayer for her grandfather, that his soul was long gone and already in Heaven, reminded God about the rest of the family, asked him to keep evil spirits from them. She prayed fervently. There had been no thunder. She blew out the candle and closed her eyes.

She was on Silma Hill, at night. A soft summer breeze. The trees had gone. The ring of stones all stood, like new, like old. It was dark, a new moon, not a light in the village, no fire, no candle. Just the starlight. She looked up at the bright sky, the washes of white and yellow, the river of the Milky Way. Uncountable points of fire. She found the plough, familiar, comforting, pointing to the North Star. As she watched it shivered, quaked, rippled into movement. One by one all the stars shook themselves awake, spun around each other, cycling faster and faster. They dropped, flew towards her. She was surrounded by billions of points of flame spinning, her at the centre, faster, faster, then nothing. Blackness. All blinked out together. She was alone in nothingness. Then she saw them. Eyes. Two gold eyes staring at her from the darkness. Piercing. She ran down Silma Hill, the eyes with her all the way, stumbling, up again and running, past the manse, the kirk, through the village by the MacFarlanes, the Dalziels, the Tollbooth and the cross, to the farm but the eyes were there first, waiting at the door. She skidded to a stop, spun and ran again, back through the village, weaving, trying to escape, into gardens, over walls, through Angus Grant's barn and out again, down past McBain's place to the loch, the freezing water, Tiki Rock standing guard. Exhausted she could run no more, not another step. Back against the rock, breath coming hard, crying, her eyes red and damp, the eyes, fiery, like pools of molten gold, considered her for a second. Approached. Entered into her. Fire. Fire in her head, in her soul. She screamed.

She screamed. Woke. She wiped her face, hair stuck to her cheek by sweat, rubbed her eyes. Eyes. She screamed again. They were still there. She could still see them. Not like some after-image, like when she looked at the sun and looked away. The eyes were there, in the room with her, exactly as in her dream. She screamed again. Her bedroom door burst open, her father, Murdoch, her mother, everyone came at her call. She pointed, but already the eyes had vanished, like a candle snuffed out.

8

FRESH YELLOW LIGHT, CRISP AIR, A gorgeous spring dawn broke onto the Sangsters' farm. The sun brought little relief to Eilidh, curled up at her grandmother's feet, a jittering wreck, shaking so much her mother held her like a child, but it made no difference. Everywhere she saw the hint, the afterglow of those terrible eyes, ghostly flames haunting the air.

They were all awake, so Mrs Sangster set about breakfast. Dougie and Murdoch were outside, getting started on the day. The old woman's stories had occasionally given the children nightmares but nothing like this, and not for years. Eilidh and Murdoch were grown now. Fear of the dark had long ceased tormenting them. Mr Sangster and his son dealt with it the way they dealt with anything: if there were no obvious solution, leave the problem alone until one presented itself. Talking it over would achieve nothing. Old Mrs Sangster disagreed.

'Tell me again, my dear. Tell me everything.'

Eilidh shook her head, though the gesture seemed more a shiver of terror than stubbornness.

'It might be important.'

'It was just a dream,' said Eilidh's mother, setting out the tea.

'There's no such thing as just a dream. Eilidh.' A bony finger poked hard into her arm. So Eilidh told her again, haltingly, forcing the words out, the hill, waiting, the eyes. 'And when you woke they were still there.'

Eilidh shuddered, gripped her grandmother's legs tighter.

The old woman, lost in thought, sipped a cup of tea. 'Gah, what is that? What are you after giving me tea, woman?' Eilidh's legs kicked involuntarily. She was exhausted. 'The old tales. Gold eyes.'

'Mother,' warned Shona. 'Stop, let Eilidh get some sleep before the funeral.'

'Old, old tales,' the old woman said. 'From the earliest times. Before the religion of Rome spread through these lands, people worshipped many gods and goddesses, spirits of the trees, the water, the sun.'

Shona shook her head and returned to the kitchen where she was repairing a hole in her shawl.

'There was one goddess, Amananto, a fierce warrior, a great hunter, stronger and faster than the male deities. She was beautiful too, with piercing gold eyes, and all the gods wanted her for their own. But she would take with none of them, for she wanted one who was her equal or better, and none of the gods were up to scratch. Slowly the gods accepted that she was to forever remain a flower unplucked. Then people from another land came on their boats and brought with them their gods. These gods were different. The deities of this land were of nature: the babbling rivers, the gentle willows, the green rolling hills. These new deities were from a land of ice and rock, of iron and gold.'

Eilidh uncurled as her grandmother's voice soothed, the storyteller's rhythms rocking her. Once there had been stories before bed, kelpies and selkies, sprites and monsters.

'They were stronger and harder than any, and their leader, Hodra, was the smartest, the strongest of them all. When Hodra and Amananto met, they each saw their mirror: an equal, a male for a female, a female for a male. They fell in love. The gods of this land were outraged. She wouldn't have one of her own, but she would lie with this incomer? The insult was too much. Strong they may not have been, but they were cunning. They concocted a plan. Combining powers they flooded the lands, they whipped up mighty winds, they burned the forests and the fields. The men from over the seas were killed and as they died, their gods grew weaker and smaller. Eventually only a handful of men, not enough to fill one boat, fled taking their now spent gods with them. Amananto was broken-hearted, and in her pain she grew furious. A war erupted, her against the others, a civil war between the gods.'

She paused to drink and noticed that Shona had put down her work and was listening. Age be dammed, she still had the stuff to hold an audience. She nudged Eilidh, directed her onto the couch, let her curl up there rather than on the floor like a dog.

'She was strong, but she was alone. She lost. They bound her to a great tree at the top of a hill and they burnt her. As her body was consumed, the gods could still see her gold eyes, fierce and furious, through the flames. Watching them, never looking away, never allowing them to forget their betrayal. Soon nothing was left but a pile of ash. After, though, the gods were forever haunted by her eyes. She had been the best of them, and they had done her in. She wouldn't leave them alone. Eventually, desperate to escape her eyes, the gods themselves abandoned these lands and the people here. New gods came, then the one God, and the most ancient were forgotten. But Amananto's eyes remained, forever vigilant, forever seeking revenge on the males who had destroyed her love and then destroyed her, all through jealousy.'

'The eyes,' said Eilidh, quietly. She looked around like she might see Amananto on her grandfather's empty chair or coming in from the garden. The birds and dogs and men at work that filled the village with sound all seemed silent, as if all were listening to the story. It was truth, it was gospel. There were things in the world, Eilidh knew, things that didn't get talked about in the kirk. Her grandmother knew them, knew the eyes. She moved closer to her, the protection of touch.

'So you see, little one, though you may have seen her

eyes, do not fear them. Amananto is a goddess, a protector of women. Perhaps she has a message for you, perhaps she is just letting you know she is there, a comfort in your grief. But you should not fear her.'

Eilidh curled herself tighter, gripped her grandmother's arm harder.

9

SCATTERED SKETCHES OF THE STATUE AND bog around him, and the idol itself lying on a blanket on the table beside his reading chair. Burnett worked in methodical stages to establish its age and provenance. The area had changed hands a number of times.

Initially he tried to date the piece via the bog, but the variables were untameable. The old man must have found it quite near the surface, hinting at a recent burial: in antiquities, as in men, depth usually implied age, and vice versa. But bogs defied his reasoning. There was no method for ascertaining the age of a natural bog. Once heath began to grow, there was no further production of peat. Whether it had been there for two centuries or twenty, none could say.

That avenue blocked, he turned to the idol itself. Assuming some antiquity, three main groups could have been responsible for its creation: Heathen Celts, Christian Celts or Norsemen. It could also be Roman or belong to any one of the nations who made up the Roman army – Syrians, Spaniards, Africans – but that was less likely. The initial three groups were there for longer and so evidence of their existence more probable. For Burnett, probability was tainted, sinful. In a world of absolutes, probability had no place.

Fiona announced dinner but he dismissed her with a flap, like a cow flicking off an insect.

He quickly put the heathen Celts aside. They were well known for having idols and images of their false gods, but not a single example remained and the only sure knowledge of the Celts was from Roman sources. If it was heathen Celtic, there was no way to check.

Christian Celts also seemed unlikely. Early Christian idols would have been of Christ, Mary, perhaps a saint. Burnett's idol was clearly none of those. Furthermore, the early Christian Fathers would never have allowed an image of a female saint or the Holy Mother to show the breasts and genitals. Not Christian, he concluded, though he penned a letter to the Reverend Stewart in Aberdeenshire, whose *Manuscript on Early Christian Images* he had before him.

Scandinavian, then. The area had a long history with the Vikings. The sea loch provided shelter from storm and safe anchorage for longboats. Many local place names still resonated with the language of the Norse, such as Tiki Rock, the enormous boulder that stood guard over the narrowest point of the river running from the loch to the bay. Tiki had been their god of stone, a talisman to pray to as the ships left the safety of Abdale Loch.

Here he had a problem. Burnett knew little about Vikings and had no manuscripts at hand to use as a guide. To either confirm or rule out a Norse origin he must go to Edinburgh. Two or three times a year Burnett tried to escape Abdale for the intellectual society of the capital. The Very Reverend Reid, a friend from student days, was ensconced at the heart of the theological, political and scientific life. Through him, Burnett would be able to access whatever documents and manuscripts he needed, as well as spend a stimulating few days debating with the sharpest minds of the age. He sat back in his chair and contemplated the week ahead. Edinburgh was a not just the centre of society for him, it was also a site of pilgrimage. It was in Reid's kirk that he had first met Moira, the daughter of one of Reid's parishioners. Her profile as he gazed across the pews, the slight upturn of her nose, the defined yet soft jawline, the strands of sunshine blonde hair trickling out from under her hat. He had been hit by a thunderbolt obvious to all. Certainly to Reid who took it upon himself to set up an introduction, acting as something of a matchmaker. Whenever he visited Edinburgh he sat in that same seat in Reid's kirk and allowed his heart to open once more to Moira, whom Providence had taken from him so soon.

He reached for his birch, flexed it, brought it down with a loud thwack on his own hand. The pain coursed up his arm, blotting his mind, overwhelming his heart. He returned to his desk. To his work.

Late into the night he grafted, neither stiffening fingers nor guttering candles delaying him. In the morning, prior to the funeral, as the sun rose and lit up the kirkyard outside his window, he began his preparation for the trip. Organisation was key. What did he need to know, where could he find that information and whose help would he need to acquire it? He sent off to the Very Reverend Reid, announcing his impending visit.

All this done, hunger ambushed him and he summoned Fiona with breakfast.

10

THE VILLAGE TURNED OUT FOR THE funeral. Even Jimmy Ross was there. Usually he would be sleeping but he had to represent authority at official occasions. It was a warm spring morning and the smell of new growth drifted over the graves. Burnett stood at the head, offering prayers for the departed soul. To his right the Sangster family. To his left Fiona, Old Hughie and Malcolm. The latter two, along with Mr Sangster and Murdoch, lowered the coffin into the grave. The villagers formed a second ring around this group, bidding the old man good grace in the next world.

The graveyard wrapped around two sides of the kirk, the oldest, weather-worn stones at the back, the newer, fresher ones moving step by step away from Silma Hill. The hole was deeper than standard and, though all noticed, none mentioned it. Hughie may be past his best, but he knew what he was about: it wouldn't be too long before old Mrs Sangster joined her husband.

As Burnett reached the end of the service, he cast an eye over the grouping. The old woman, the centre of attention. The granddaughter, hair over her face, hiding behind her mother. Shaking, quivering. She was Fiona's age but showed none of the maturity. Spared the birch, he thought. A common mistake. Next the two male Sangsters, good enough workers but far from the pinnacle of the Lord's creation. To his left, he saw Fiona making eyes at someone, trying to attract their attention. Must be the daughter, Burnett guessed. The two of them were friends, though what Fiona saw in that simpleton he didn't know. An insect flitted by and the Sangster girl nearly jumped into the grave in fright.

He shook his head and a memory returned to him. He was standing at the head of another grave when a robin had flown past and settled on the gravestone. Snow lay heavy and was filling the hole before he could finish the service. That grave stood off to his right, closer to the kirk wall. The village had turned out then as well, to see Moira pass into the next world. The bitterness of that winter caught at his heart. Moira's parents had come through from Edinburgh. Burnett felt again his resentment of them, the jealousy. That was the last time he'd seen them. Moira was his memory, his grief and he would not share it with anyone. He felt the snow flurry in his soul. One long winter. He looked up from the book. The service finished, rushed to the end. It was done.

Burnett shut himself inside the kirk, Fiona led the mourners across the grass. It was a village tradition that after a funeral a wake was held in the manse. Burnett hated the custom, started before his day, but his wife had continued it during the short time she was with him and he had never found sufficient excuse to end it. He stayed out of it, left it to Fiona. Entertaining was a woman's responsibility, after all.

Fiona had set everything up outside. The layout of the manse would mean splitting people into different rooms, whereas outside they could be one large group. Tables and chairs were limited in number so boxes, and anything with a flat surface was covered with cushions, blankets, tea and ale depending on immediate needs. Etiquette was clear: Fiona would look after the bereaved family, everyone else could help themselves. There was plenty to go round.

After a respectful silence, the hum of gossip, of villagers together, spending time with each other. It was shaping to be a beautiful day, the faint smell of salt carried in from the sea mixing with spring-fresh grass, the heat enough for shirtsleeves.

Children ran around playing tag, hide and seek, whatever game they thought up. The odd burst of adult laughter broke cover, quickly muffled. Groups formed and broke, mixing, some open, some more secretive, confidences passing between them. Jimmy Ross moved around the group hoping for gossip, a secret or a mystery that might enliven his routine work but the people of Abdale were careful of what they said in front of the law. Fiona moved between everyone, returning to the Sangsters, balancing duties and responsibilities in a practised way. If it weren't for the uniform black mourning cloth, it could almost be a holiday.

Almost.

There was something wrong with Eilidh. Once everyone was suitably fed and watered, Fiona found her wedged protectively between her mother and grandmother. She topped up the grandmother's ale, did the same for Dougie, Murdoch and Malcolm. 'Is everything all right? Eilidh, are you all right?'

Eilidh looked at her, startled. 'She had a bad night,' said Shona, 'that's all.'

'A bad night?'

'She saw the eyes,' her grandmother butted in. Eilidh flinched. Shona and Dougie rounded on Mrs Sangster, unspoken reprimands in their eyes. She ignored them.

'The what?' said Malcolm.

'The eyes. The gold eyes.'

He shrugged, looked at Fiona. She had no idea either. They waited for her to explain. Old Mrs Sangster, with Murdoch's help, pulled herself upright and wandered off without another word. It was time for attention. Fiona topped up Murdoch's ale some more. 'How are you?'

'Aye, fine,' he said. 'You know.'

She nodded, though in reality she didn't. Her father was all the family she had ever had. Her mother's family were presumably dead. Burnett had never confirmed this but the one time she had found the courage to ask, he had beaten her.

Mentioning her mother to him was like provoking a bull and she never dared again. Fiona's birth was a line in history that would not be crossed. Moira was a ghost who stood between them, a chill in his heart, an emptiness in hers. Absence she knew all too well, but grief she had been spared. 'What's the matter with Eilidh? What did your grandmother mean about eyes?'

'Eilidh woke up screaming. Some nonsense about eyes. She's been like that all day.'

'Eyes?'

'There were eyes in her dream and when she woke she thought she could still see them.' He drank. 'Granny's not helping, filling her head with ancient gods and ghosts and whatnot.'

The crowd was thinning out, the food and drink all but done, people drifting home, back to work, things to be done, jobs that couldn't wait. A shout caught their attention, stopped the flow. The old woman was standing in the manse door, waving something.

'Devils! Devils!' she shouted. 'In the Minister's own house! Devils!' She had the wooden icon raised over her head. Another, louder shout. Burnett ran up, pushed through the crowd, ripped the statue from her frail hands.

'Devils! Look, Eilidh, look at the eyes. Gold eyes!'

Eilidh's scream arrested everything. She ran off, Malcolm, the quickest to react, chasing after her.

'Black magic!' the old woman shouted.

'Silence, you old hag,' Burnett yelled over her. 'This is nothing of the sort.'

'What is it then? False idols in the Minister's house!'

'Is that what my father found yesterday?' said Mr Sangster, taking a step towards Burnett.

'Yes,' said Burnett. 'It is an antiquarian find and I am studying it for presentation to the Society.'

'Oh aye, valuable is it?' Mr Sangster said. 'Found by my

father on my land.'

'And given to me.'

'What! What are you saying! My poor Rab discovered this totem? When? Where?'

'Granny,' said Murdoch. 'Calm down. He found it in the bog yesterday when he was digging. He brought it here, I saw him from the top field, and then he went back to the bog and—'

'See,' said Burnett. 'Freely given.'

'He dug it up,' the old woman said, 'and then died. You found him in the bog. He dug up this symbol of the Devil and then died. Witchcraft! Black magic! This image is cursed!'

Burnett turned to Mr Sangster. 'Please take this mad woman away from here. I will not have this superstition spouted outside my home, on holy ground. This is not the dark ages. This is the eighteenth century. The rest of you can go, too,' he said, addressing the crowd. 'We all have serious work to attend to. This is a solemn day, not a day for frivolities or the rantings of a mad old woman.'

Old Mrs Sangster faced him, curled finger raised. 'That idol is cursed, Burnett. Burn that today or there will be trouble. The evil spirit has been loosed. My own granddaughter saw it last night. It walks free and more death and destruction will follow in its wake.'

'Go home, lunatic, and keep your drivel to yourself. This is a piece of historical interest and nothing more. Spirits do not live in objects. Only children and Papists believe that kind of claptrap. Now leave. Your husband is buried. I have done my duty to your family and you are trampling on my hospitality.'

'Now, Minister,' said Jimmy Ross.

'Now what, Jimmy? An old woman breaks into my house in front of your very eyes and you do nothing.'

'And what would you have me do, Minister? Perhaps you would like me to send for Sheriff Dawkins to investigate?'

For a moment Burnett was knocked off his sure ground. 'Investigate what? We have the criminal here. Clap her in the

Tollbooth and have done with it.'

'All the same, I think Dawkins would like to be involved.'

'I don't give a damn what Dawkins would like, this is my parish. Your job is to catch criminals. Here is one. Are you going to do your job?' With one last look of disgust at Ross and the Sangsters, Burnett went into the manse and slammed the door.

Mrs Sangster wasn't done. 'Unnatural, I tell you. Lunatic he may call me but my eyes are open. I know the marks of witchcraft when I see them.'

'Missus Sangster,' said Ross. 'Are you making a formal accusation of witchcraft?'

Witchcraft. The word ran round an incredulous crowd. It had been nearly three generations since the trials and burnings. Ross's question arrested her. She knew how the fever spread, how one accusation led to another, and each accusation had a habit of making its way back to the accuser. 'Something's afoot in Abdale,' she said, picking her words more carefully. 'I don't rightly know what yet, but mark my words, young Jimmy Ross, there's evil in that house.' With that she lowered her black shawl over her face to make a mourning veil, ending all further discussion, and made her way home.

The crowd – reformed around the spectacle – broke up once more. Fiona was left alone with the debris of the day. She didn't know which way to turn: her friend, Murdoch or her duty at home, to clean up the mess. Watching retreating backs, she sadly stacked dishes and took everything inside.

11

THE NIGHT WAS LONG AS FIONA rewound the day. Each time she came near sleep another scene would play and the memory would make her fidget, spasm with shame. She rose early the next morning and hastened through her duties. Once all the floors were scrubbed, the breakfast things washed, lunch prepared and the washing whipping in the wind, she wrapped up the leftover food from the funeral and readied herself.

She hadn't seen her father since the end of the funeral. He had eaten in his study, hadn't slept in his bed. When she had knocked with his food, he hadn't answered, so she left the tray outside. Later a plate, rubble of the meal and an empty glass stood in their place. She wondered if he was lost in his study of that idol, or if Mrs Sangster had troubled him. Both were guilty, but Fiona knew where the villagers' sympathy would be. Did her father's behaviour tar her as well?

Her basket of food for the Sangsters on the crook of her arm, she left the manse. The wind had got up since the day before and there was a chill in the air, a reminder that summer had yet to come. It seemed everyone was out, waiting for her to pass. Angus Grant and Old McBain stood chatting by the cross, Mrs MacFarlane and Mrs Dalziel in their gardens folding blankets. Jimmy Ross sat against the door of the Tollbooth. She greeted everyone and they replied sure enough, but no further. Everyone was watching her, waiting to see if the gossips' predictions would come true, waiting for something to happen. Even the boys returning from Mrs McGowan's schoolroom were quiet, as if they too sensed something. None of the games, the cries and names, chasing and fights. She was being judged.

At the Sangsters' farm, Murdoch was in the yard sharpening tools, chickens pecking around his feet. She couldn't see any of the rest of his family.

'Hey, sweetheart,' she said.

'Oh. Morning.'

'How is everyone today?'

'Not great, you know. After—'

'Of course. I came to see Eilidh. She looked terrible yesterday and I want to see if she's better.'

'I'm – I'm not so sure that's a good idea.'

'Why not?'

'Granny.'

'You mean she doesn't want to see me because of my father?'

'I'm not sure it would be a good idea for her to see anyone.'

Fiona couldn't find a way to counter him. The dull grate of stone on blade hung between them. She kicked out at a chicken that took an interest in her boot. 'How is Eilidh, then?'

'It's hell in there, to be honest. That's why I'm out here.'

'Could you get Eilidh to come out?'

'I think she's sleeping—'

'When are you up on the hill again? I could make us another lunch.'

'Not sure.'

The crack of a slammed door echoed as Shona came out of the house. 'You've a neck,' she said to Fiona.

'Morning, Missus Sangster. I brought some food from yesterday.' She proffered the basket. 'I just came to see Eilidh, to see if she was—'

'Aye, we all know who you came to see. But no Burnetts are welcome around here no more.'

'Please, Missus Sangster—'

'Never been so offended.'

Tears pricked their way out. 'I'm sorry, Missus Sangster, it was wrong.'

'Aye, well, until that man comes down here and apologises, you can consider yourself unwelcome.' Murdoch kept his eyes on the scythe, whetstone along the blade. The door opened again and the old woman appeared.

'Beware the eyes, Fiona Burnett. You have the Devil in your house.' Behind her Eilidh stood gaunt, hair straggly and unbrushed. She turned and ran, dropping her basket, ran all the way home, tears, out of breath, past the villagers, the gossip seconds behind her, village legends forming in her wake.

12

MURDOCH BLEW OUT THE CANDLE AND closed his eyes, but his mind wouldn't give him peace. Fiona's face, crumpling in hurt, the tears, the lips he'd kissed, those berry lips trembling. He could have said something. Could have done something. No. Their relationship was secret and this was family, after all. And she wasn't family yet.

He couldn't bear staring into the darkness, avoiding the memory, so he went outside. It was warm now the wind had waned. He stretched, made his back creak, forced the stiffness out of his shoulders. He'd done little in the way of work the day before and his body was tightening. Built up energy, bottled. He needed to burn off spirits.

The village was quiet so deep into the night. Dawn over the far banks of Loch Abdale was an hour away and every home quiet. These houses were warm, the presence of people inside giving vitality to the stones and wood. Even the kirk, imposing and dark as he strolled by, seemed that night to flow with the life of the village. All those Sundays, weddings, christenings, funerals, all the villagers buried beneath it.

A candle was burning in the manse. Burnett's study. Up all night with that idol no doubt. A chill as he remembered his grandmother's words. During the day her stories were fictions designed to entertain and unsettle. He'd had a lifetime of them and had marked it a stage in his progression towards manhood when he ceased to believe in them. Here, standing in the shadows, the graveyard to his left, the solid mass of the manse before him, the silhouette of Silma Hill rising behind it. What if she were right? Inside that room, inside the home of his beloved, sat an evil talisman, some work of the Devil that had brought about his grandfather's death. Was the Devil in Abdale?

As the thought dripped, the candle in the study guttered, shadows dancing on the corner of wall visible to him. He watched as it dimmed, darkened. A force grabbed him and he turned his back on the manse, ran fast as he could, by Angus Grant's barn, down the hill towards the loch. He had run this way many times as a child playing games, chasing, being chased by friends, by angry adults, by imaginary monsters. The fear that singed his feet as they slapped the road was real, not the pretend terror of childhood games.

He stopped at the loch edge and let his breath catch up. He felt much better. Pushing his muscles, stretching his limbs, he had outrun his fear, outpaced his anxiety. Soft waves rubbed the shore, the calmness of the surface, the repetitive lullaby of the water. Old McBain's ferry rose and fell gently alongside the short jetty, the cable stretching to the far shore swaying heavily, hung between the oak on that side and, on this, Tiki Rock, the egg-shaped marker showing where the loch ended and the pathway to the sea began. It was an arbitrary point, he knew, just a narrowing, a bringing together of the banks, but for centuries it had marked the end of Abdale. Vikings, his grandmother had told him, believed it was a god, a watcher with the power to protect those who harboured here and paid sufficient devotion. As their boats sailed out to sea they would arc a fiery arrow over the rock, a symbol of their respect, a request for continued protection.

The sweat dried on his back. He would never sleep. A bit more of a stroll, he thought, and then I'll get back up the hill. The beasts would need checking, the dry dyke needed finishing and the peat needed digging. He would be spending a lot more time around Silma Hill, many more chances for secret lunches. A grin before he remembered. Damn it all, he thought. This wasn't his fight. Family or not, this was just two old people locking horns. It had nothing to do with Fiona and him. He would find a way to see her, to apologise. He would make it up to her, somehow.

Aimlessly stepping along the waterline, the shingle shifting under his boots, each step unbalancing him, dragging him into the stroke of the loch. A pang told him he was hungry. Old McBain was awake and the smell of porridge carried on the wind from his house. When Murdoch was a kid he had often played down here and Old McBain would let him clamber over the ferry, teach him to tie knots, show him how to bait a fish line. Murdoch hadn't been down to see him in years. Too busy, too old for playing. They exchanged a few words on Sundays in the kirk but Old McBain was never much of a talker and Murdoch never knew what to say to him beyond the weather and the ferry. He thought about chapping on the door, a wave of nostalgia brought on by the smell, but before he could make up his mind, something moved.

On top of Tiki Rock stood a figure. In the darkness it was impossible to make out anything more than the vaguest outline. An echo of his earlier terror reverberated but he forced it silent, the scent of porridge anchoring him. Carefully now, trying not to make noise, he moved away from the loch. Unbearable sound of shingle but the four or five steps it took him to reach grass provoked no reaction. Quicker now but stealthily, as if hunting, he closed the distance, darted across the open road that led to the jetty and ducked into the tree line. Convinced he hadn't been seen, he moved through the branches and roots until he was almost at the rock.

Dawn was beginning to seep over the rolling farmland at the far end of the loch and the faintest hint of light was enough to clarify his quarry. It was a young woman, her long dark hair dancing in the salt breeze. She was crouched on top of the rock. A flare in him, bright and hot, as the woman stood. Naked. Her back was to him but he could clearly see the silhouette profile of a breast. A stirring in his britches. He rubbed his hand slowly over his hardness. Who was it? Mary Dalziel? Lorna McGowan? He looked around to make sure no one else was there, that he couldn't be seen, that Jimmy Ross wasn't making an unexpected effort to do his job. Which village girl was it had a secret life, exposing herself under the stars? Who was looser in morals than he had suspected?

The woman raised her arms above her head and began to dance, slow, sensual. The position made her breasts more prominent and the dance caused such movement that Murdoch could no longer contain himself. He rubbed faster, harder, and warm liquid burst over the inside of his thigh. He wiped sweat from his brow on his sleeve, shifted his position as the wetness cooled uncomfortably. She was still dancing and as Murdoch watched, his breathing subsiding, she turned gracefully, raising her face to the breaking day.

He gasped, stood involuntarily, cracking his head on a branch and dislodging sleeping birds who filled the sky with startled song. He stepped out of the tree line. The woman had noticed nothing and was still dancing. He couldn't believe it. The shock. Eilidh. The desire to run strong in him again, but he fought it. He had to get her home before anyone saw.

He called out her name. No response. He tried again, raising his voice. Nothing. He didn't want to call too loudly in case Old McBain heard and looked out. He circled the great rock looking for a clue as to how Eilidh had climbed it, but saw nothing. This rock was more than twice his height and the sides worn smooth as glass by lifetimes of wind and rain. How had she got up there? Following the steps of her dance he kept himself in her sightline, naming her. The sun was visible on the horizon, a thin slice warning him. The village would be waking. In frustration he picked a small stone from the ground and, aiming carefully, hit her leg. She stopped moving momentarily, then continued her dance. He chose a bigger stone and tried again, this time hitting her just above the place he was trying to avoid looking. She stopped again, slowly lowered her head in his direction and opened her eyes. Murdoch felt something pierce his stomach at the exact point the rock had hit Eilidh, and the pain made him double over, but he didn't break eye contact. His gaze was held by the fierce gold eyes staring back at him.

'Eilidh, in God's name, wake up.' A pause, the eyes watched him. Then, as if in slow motion, her body crumpled and she fell forward off the rock. He caught her, sat her on the ground. He yanked his shirt off and put it on her. He was much taller than her and when he pulled her vertical it hung almost to her knees. She was out cold, unresponsive to his words. He picked her up, checked her modesty was covered and set off through the trees, to get to the house the back way. With luck they would make it without being seen. Climbing, he looked back at the rock. As the new day washed down the loch he could still make out the two gold eyes, exactly where he'd last seen them, above Tiki Rock. Then the sun reached them and they faded. He ran home, Eilidh a dead weight in his arms.

13

THE FEW SECONDS BETWEEN THE COCKEREL'S crow and reality, if that was death, perhaps it was something to welcome. Dougie Sangster yawned and scratched his hairy stomach. Just another minute. The pigs could wait for their slop. The cockerel had sounded different. Almost human. Had he been dreaming? Then it came again.

'Dougie!' It was Shona. What was wrong with her? With all the women in this family?

'What is it?'

'It's Eilidh, she's not in her bed. Neither's Murdoch.'

He scooped his shirt off the floor and ran through, checking the rooms. 'She can't have got far, not in her state.'

'Maybe Jimmy Ross has seen her.'

'Only thing he'll have seen is the back of his eyelids. Don't tell the old woman. I'll look for her.'

'Tell me what?' said old Mrs Sangster, appearing in the doorway.

'Away back inside and find something to keep you out of trouble.'

Shona ran out into the road, a few steps towards Ben Morvyn, a few steps to the village, ran back to Dougie who held her firm. 'They'll be fine. I'll find them. I'll go through the village first. If they're towards Ben Morvyn likely no one will see them. You wait here in case they return.' He splashed water on his face and marched off, scattering chickens before him. At the Tollbooth there were no signs of life. He stalked like a hunter, listening for unnatural sounds, jumping walls, climbing over fences, looking in gardens and behind outhouses. Down the burn road by the kirk and the manse, he ran to the loch, circled back up by Angus Grant's and once more through the village. Shutters and doors were opening.

Shona was carving a trench into the path from road to the house. Where were they? Step, turn. Were they together? Step, turn. What had happened? Step, turn. Why were they gone? Step, turn. What was wrong with Eilidh? Step, turn. Where was Dougie? Step, turn.

'Ma,' a voice from behind the house. Murdoch coming out of the trees with Eilidh in his arms.

Shona bolted to her children. 'Eilidh? Eilidh? What's the matter with her?'

'Hold on,' said Murdoch. 'Can't you see she's not decent? Let me get her inside.' They followed him into her room, where he laid her on the bed, put a blanket over her.

'What the hell were you two up to?' said Dougie, running in.

'I couldn't sleep,' said Murdoch. 'Just before sun up I went down to the loch. I found her there.' He paused, pushing his guilt aside. 'She was on top of Tiki Rock. Dancing. Naked.'

Dougie swore. 'Eilidh,' he said. 'What were you doing?'

'She's asleep,' said Murdoch. 'She didn't recognise me, didn't see me. I had to… she never woke the whole way.'

'She's burning up,' said Shona. 'Everyone out.' She hustled them through to the kitchen, got a bowl of water and a rag and went back to tend her daughter.

'Did anyone see?' said Dougie.

'No. Old McBain was up but he never came out, and there's no one in the woods at this time.'

'Not a word of this to anyone. I'll have no gossip about this family.' He looked around the house, looking for something to do, a problem to solve, someone to blame. 'Right, the day's started and neither of us know a damn thing of use to Eilidh, so let's get to work. You finished that dyke yet?'

'Not yet.'

'Well then.'

He would love some breakfast and a nap but he followed his father outside. A hand stopped him. Mr Sangster didn't notice and turned the corner without looking back. Murdoch faced his grandmother. There was a greedy look in her eye, the kind a dog has as it watches its master prepare food. He knew what she wanted, knew she would get it out of him. Better to get it over with.

'What did you see?' she said. 'What aren't you telling?' He swallowed, paused. Acknowledgment made it real. Inside his head it could be imagination. As soon as he gave it voice, he would no longer have control. 'Eyes? Gold eyes?' He nodded. 'Where? Watching?'

'Watching me. They were in her eyes. When she looked at me.'

'In her eyes? Did they leave her? Are they still in her?'

'Aye, they left. When she fell, they stayed above the rock.'

'Did they follow you?'

'They disappeared into the sunlight. Do you know what it is? What's going on?'

She winked at him, tapped her nose. He wasn't in the mood, not today. He pulled the door and set off for Silma Hill. He had barely reached the road when the door opened again. Mrs Sangster needed more information and knew better than any in Abdale how to get it. First stop: MacFarlane's inn.

14

BURNETT SPENT THE REMAINDER OF THE week in his study working on the idol and made as much progress as he could at home. There were books he needed to see and people he needed to interrogate before he could reach any sound conclusions, and neither were to be found in Abdale. He would depart for Edinburgh the following morning. He would have gone earlier but the Sabbath cycle continued irrespective of man's desires. He had a job to do and it wouldn't be right for him to travel straight after the service.

Fiona had suffered through a miserable few days. The whole village knew of the Sangsters' verdict and took sides. Buying eggs and milk meant the whisper of disapproval and angular silences. Friends like Mary Dalziel gave her pitying looks, secret smiles, but that only made things worse. From Murdoch, not a word. She saw him up on Silma Hill working on the dyke, minding the beasts, and it took all the strength she had not to load up the basket and run to see him. He had made it clear on which side he stood. She picked at leftovers and sought something else to clean.

Sunday ended the isolation of the manse. The divided village had no choice but to come together at the kirk. Burnett delivered exactly the sermon he had prepared the week before, extolling the virtues of reason over superstition, taking Romans 15: 4 as his starting point. "For whatsoever things were written aforetime were written for our learning, that we through patience and comfort of the scriptures might have hope." He was aware of some of the mumblings and rumblings in the village, and Old McBain and Old Hughie kept him up-to-date with whatever gossip they picked up, but the kirk was outside and above terrestrial concerns. They could bump gums all they wanted Monday to Saturday but come Sunday they sat on his pews, listened to his words and heeded his lessons. When he penned the sermon he couldn't have known how appropriate it would turn out to be, but he felt the Lord had been guiding his hand. There was no place for superstition in Abdale, not while he was the authority there.

Sat in her usual place Fiona was all too aware of the atmosphere behind her. The villagers were taking the sermon as a direct assault. Sitting in the kirk and being harangued as sinners they were used to. Being chided as stubborn, ignorant children stuck in their gullets. This was an attack and Fiona could sense the lines being drawn across the pews. Reason over superstition. Rationality over idolatry. Science over folk myths. Burnetts over Sangsters. She had been cut off from the gossip, but she knew talk had not been idle. She could sense it, the tension of knowledge in the room, the ties of agreement.

The service over, she stood with her father as usual shaking hands with everyone as they left. Burnett received the respect his position demanded. He asked for no more and got no more. They passed Fiona like she was a ghost. As the Sangsters' turn came she thought she was going to be sick. Mr Sangster made vague gestures in their direction but the old woman marched by, arms folded. Murdoch came sheepishly after, touching Fiona's hand for a second before running after his family. She bit her lip hard. Only when the acid waves fell back did she realise Eilidh and her mother hadn't been there. All other worries cascaded away and she hastened to Mr Sangster. The villagers had congregated into cliques in the kirkyard.

'Please, Mister Sangster,' she began, 'I know you have no wish to speak with me, but please tell me how Eilidh is? She's not here today and I fear she must be very sick.'

'Eilidh's fine,' he said, shortly. 'She just needs some rest.' He stalked off, Murdoch trailing behind. The old woman stayed.

'You, Fiona. What have you seen?'

'What have I seen?'

'Aye, what have you seen? At night. When you're alone.'

'What have I seen? Nothing. What do you mean?'

'Nothing? You have seen nothing at all?' The old woman grabbed her arm and pulled her close, so they were inches from each other. Fiona felt like her very soul was being examined. 'Aye, no lie in there, sure enough, you have seen nothing. Curious, that. Right curious.'

'What are you talking about?'

'Either you already know or you will know soon enough, Fiona Burnett.' She left Fiona standing on the grass. Her father was already in his study. He called to her as she closed the front door. She used the time offered by hanging up her hat and removing her shawl to compose herself. She found him straightening his papers and putting them into his leather satchel. His hat, cloak and gloves were laid on a chair, ready to be worn.

'Tomorrow I have to go to Edinburgh on business so pack me a bag. I'm planning to be back on Saturday.'

'Edinburgh? On Kirk business?'

'No,' he said, sharply. Who was she to interrogate him? 'I am incapable of completing my studies so far from learned civilisation, and so I must depart. Assuming no one else dies in the next few days, I am sure the village will not get up to too much mischief in my absence. Apart from the mad woman. Still, the Lord cannot be too long in gathering her into His arms. Now, while I am gone there will be no skimping on your duties. This is not a holiday.'

'No, sir,' gritted teeth.

'And I will be locking this door. That statue is too valuable to transport and I do not want that lunatic trying to get her hands on it. Have you been to see that friend of yours, by the way?'

'I haven't seen her,' Fiona replied, not answering his question, but not quite lying. He nodded, seemingly satisfied.

Fiona went to her father's bedroom. As she packed, she thought about the days ahead. Not a holiday? Any time out from under his gaze was a holiday. Her duties were done by late morning and with no meals to prepare for him, the time would be her own. But to what end? Until Murdoch came and apologised, she was alone.

15

THAT NIGHT BROUGHT A NEW EXPERIENCE for Jimmy Ross. For the first time in twenty years he was kept awake.

The youngest of six sons of a farmer from Dunklay, a village to the south of Abdale, Ross had quit home in search of employment, moving first to Glentrow then to Abdale. The nocturnal nature of his work put a temporal barrier between him and the villagers and the usual means of entering a community – marriage – had never happened for him. No one wants a man who sleeps all day and lives in a tollbooth, however empty the cells may be.

As the sun set behind the peak of Ben Morvyn, red soaked through the clouds over the ocean, he made his rounds of the village. In his pocket he carried a few strips of dried beef on which he chewed as he strolled. He made the same round every night as people were turning in, his presence reassuring them that, as they slept, their security was guaranteed. He knew his reputation but didn't resent it. Folk often dismiss what they can't see and by its very nature, his work went unseen. He nodded greetings, exchanged pleasantries as he passed. The beef had a salty, smoky flavour that aroused his palate, stimulated his nose. He clasped his hands behind his back and rolled his shoulders. Bed would be welcome.

The last light was seeping around the slopes of the mountain when he reached the loch. Alone on the shore, McBain by habit long since asleep, he sat on the jetty and lit his pipe. The blue tobacco smoke curled up and drifted over the dark water, the scent of cherry wood mixing with the pines on the far shore. His life may not be what he dreamed as a boy but for all that he couldn't complain. He puffed away in the deepening darkness.

A sound, the crystal tinkle of shingle shifting. He rose at the end of the jetty and peered onto the shore but he could see nothing, the molten glow of the pipe bowl affecting his vision. He tapped the pipe out into the water and slid it into his pouch, waited a few moments while his eyes adjusted, then made his way back to dry land, his feet echoing through the wooden boards. On the shoreline he stopped, listened, but there was nothing. An animal of some sort. He looked out at the water again, less welcoming now the sun had gone, now the pleasant warmth of pipe smoke had dissipated. A story about kelpies from his childhood unfurled before him but he shook it away. It wouldn't do for the nightwatchman to scare himself in the dark. He followed the path up the hill back into the village. As he passed the kirk a child's laugh broke from the kirkyard. He stopped, held his breath. Silence. Emptiness. But then again, a laugh. It happened again, it was real. He shivered. Should he run back to the Tollbooth and light a torch? Should he go into the kirkyard and investigate? He waited, breathing shallow. If nothing more happened before he counted to one hundred, he would call it imagination and go to bed. His fingers found his pipe and packet, began packing the bowl, forty-five, forty-six, a laugh, again. Over there, by the kirk itself. Surprised to find his pipe in his hands, he put it away and stepped over the low dyke into the field of graves. To his right he could just make out the slight mound of Mr Sangster's grave but the sound had come from deeper in the kirkyard. He made his way carefully around the stones, moving into the older part, dates counting back through the history of Abdale, a record of all who had died there. All those bodies, skeletons, every person who had lived and died in Abdale under his feet. He pinched the skin on the back of his hand. Stop that. Not a child. He reached the kirk wall and followed it, keeping his fingers in contact with the rough stone until it ended. He held his breath, out, in, out, now, and stepped around the corner. A figure, darker than the night, swept around the other side of the kirk. He took chase, walking fast rather than running, swerving around gravestones, sticking close to the wall. He circled the kirk but there was nothing. He ran down the burn road following it behind Abdale until it curled back into the village. He reached the cross, the heart of Abdale. He leaned against it, catching his wind when a scream, long, high and fearful flew out into the night. Turning, getting a sense of the direction. The Dalziels. Running again, he reached their house as a second scream rang out. He pounded on the door, announcing himself. Malcolm swung it open. Ross pushed in.

Mr and Mrs Dalziel were through the house, candles flickering down the passage. Mary was lying on the floor, fainted.

'What happened?'

'She saw something, something in the window,' said Mr Dalziel. 'We were asleep when she screamed first but here the second time. She pointed at the window and screamed, then fainted cold.'

'Did you see anything?'

He shook his head. Mrs Dalziel was beside her daughter, her head raised onto her lap. 'Eyes,' she said softly. 'Fiery eyes.'

'Mister Ross.'

Jimmy turned and saw Mr MacFarlane, the innkeeper. 'Yes?'

'If you can come. Something's happened.'

He nodded, told Mr Dalziel he would be back and followed Mr MacFarlane outside. Along the road the wild flowers that grew had been beheaded, the verge strewn with purple, white and yellow petals. As they neared the inn he realised the ground was wet, frothy puddles forming. 'What's this?'

'All my ale,' said Mr MacFarlane. 'Someone has emptied every barrel onto the road.' He stored the barrels in an outhouse in the back of the inn. Someone had opened the gate, unlocked the outhouse door, moved the full barrels outside, broken them open and emptied each one. Gallons of ale flowed over the rough ground.

'Who would do this?' said Ross.

'Who could do this?' said MacFarlane. 'I have the only key – the lock hasn't been forced – and it takes two men to move a barrel.'

The streets were filling with people, the commotion at the Dalziel's house had awakened them and the stench of beer hung over the village. Ross left MacFarlane and moved among the villagers. People brought torches and so the extent of the flood and the flower slaughter became clearer. Rumour ran with the beer and soon he was getting garbled versions of things he already knew. He decided to take charge and apply some logic to the situation. 'Everyone gather around the cross. Everyone to the cross so we can all hear everything. No more gossiping. Come on. Move. To the cross.' Curiosity rather than his authority moved them and in a few minutes he was addressing a large crowd.

'Right. Here is what I know. Someone was running around the kirkyard. I chased them but they disappeared. Then Mary Dalziel saw someone at her window. At about the same time someone – more probably two men – emptied Mister MacFarlane's barrels. Does anyone have anything else to report? I don't want gossip or rumour, just fact. Have you seen or heard anything else tonight? Do you have any information about who may be responsible?'

Before anyone could answer the kirk bells clapped out a peal. In the darkness, the noise echoing back from Ben Morvyn and Silma Hill. The crowd scattered, some running for home but most ran towards the kirk, Ross with them. When they arrived Burnett and Fiona were coming out of the manse, the bells still clanging.

'Who in the Lord's name is doing that?' Burnett shouted

but no one answered. The kirk doors were bolted shut. The crowd parted for him and closed again as he put the huge iron key in the lock. Still the bells rang. They flowed into the kirk, the torches casting shadows around the pillars, strange shapes high into the roof. Burnett marched to the belfry, the mob hard behind him, still the bells ringing. He threw the curtain aside but the room was empty, just two ropes pumping up and down in a steady rhythm, still the bells ringing.

16

THE NEXT MORNING BURNETT SUMMONED ROSS to the manse. Seated behind his desk, waiting, he considered his packed bags by the door. He would not admit it aloud but the events of the night before had unsettled him. Not because of the bell ringing which was easily explained by science – a strong high-level wind off the ocean moved the bells – unusual but not particular cause for alarm. Rather he was startled by the speed with which his parishioners had leapt at supernatural causes. Had the old woman's cries of 'Devil' been heeded? Like a smouldering fire, he had to stamp it out. Edinburgh would be postponed for a week. Seven days of firefighting, a well-penned sermon on Sunday and he would be able to leave without the village falling apart in his absence. First, he had to get Ross under control.

Ross sat at his own desk, the heel of his palms pushed into his eyes. The bells had continued ringing until dawn. Angus Grant had tried to stop them by grabbing one of the ropes and it lifted him clear off the ground, nearly ripping his arms out in the process. Ross had returned to interview the Dalziels and the MacFarlanes but he had already learned everything they knew. He needed sleep. He lifted his hat off the floor where it had fallen and, pausing only to plunge his face in a pail of water, made his way to the manse.

Fiona showed him into the study. Burnett remained seated, nodded at the chair opposite him. 'So. What do you know?'

'No more than I told you a few hours ago.'

'And what is your next step?'

'I will write an initial report on the events last night. Then I will begin questioning people.'

'You will write your report before you have questioned anyone?'

'I have spoken to the Dalziels and the MacFarlanes, the people directly involved. Yourself.'

'But you do not know what new information may be out there waiting for you. Surely it would be premature to report now?'

'I know enough to report, just not enough to draw conclusions.'

'Dawkins will want conclusions.'

'The Sheriff will want to know.'

'If you wait until you have gathered more information, you can send a better report. Maybe even find the culprits yourself. Think about that. The first crime in Abdale in a generation and you solve it by yourself. Dawkins wouldn't even need to bother coming all this way.'

It took two days for Ross to speak to everyone. Each night there were more sightings of golden eyes floating disembodied, laughter in the darkness, movement in the shadows. As he suspected, no one knew anything, but they all had theories. He spent his days questioning, writing, collating, his nights patrolling. Sleep came in short bursts, an hour or two. Was it exhaustion that made him put off interviewing the Sangsters until last, or because they would be the most difficult?

The evening of the second day he made his way to their farm. There was an atmosphere around the house, unwelcoming. The chickens pecked the ground long after they should be locked away from hungry foxes. The shutters were closed even though light still shone on Abdale. He banged on the door, announcing himself, waited. After a moment it opened a crack and Mr Sangster looked out. 'What?'

'I need to speak to you all.'

'Later.'

'I'm sorry but I need to do it now. I have spoken to everyone else.'

'Will it take long?'

'It shouldn't.'

'Very well.' He opened the door wider, admitted Ross into the kitchen. The family were all present, Shona and Eilidh on the couch, Mrs Sangster in her chair, Murdoch at the table. The remains of a meal not yet cleared. Dougie took his seat across from his son and motioned for Ross to sit. No one offered him tea or ale. They looked as he felt, eyes ringed with sleep, skin pale. Eilidh was curled under a blanket, only her eyes visible to him. Shona stroked her arm through the blanket. He cleared his throat.

'As you know I am compiling a report for the Sheriff in Glentrow of everything that happened on Sunday night. Before I send it I want to ascertain if there is any further information I should include.'

'What have you learned from others?' asked Mr Sangster.

'Little of note. Everyone was inside asleep. Apart from the Dalziels and the MacFarlanes no one saw anything. The first most knew was hearing others in the street.'

'And we're no different,' said Shona.

'Others have seen the eyes?' said Mrs Sangster.

Dougie gave his mother a cold look.

'Yes. Last night Lorna McGowan reported seeing them in the twilight as she returned from the outhouse.'

'And Mary Dalziel. All young girls,' Shona said, almost to herself.

'You said at the funeral that Eilidh too had seen the… had the same experience.'

'Just once,' said Dougie, firmly. 'The night my father passed on. Nothing since then.'

'And no one else has seen anything? People moving around

outside after dark? Strange noises? Anything unusual?'

'No. Nothing. Everything in this house is normal. Now, Jimmy, it is late.' Mr Sangster stood and opened the door.

'Of course.' Ross took one last look around the family, the tension, something clearly hidden. He lingered on Eilidh. Shona wrapped an arm over her protectively. 'Thank you for your time. Good night.'

He had delayed as Burnett wanted but found nothing. He quickly concluded his report and while doing another round of the village, left the packet on Old McBain's porch for the mail coach in the morning. Nothing had happened by the time he returned to the Tollbooth so he climbed into his bed and was asleep before he had taken his second boot off.

17

BURNETT LOOKED OUT AT HIS CONGREGATION. Ross's report had been sent but so far Dawkins hadn't arrived in Abdale. Maybe they would be spared. The week had ended quietly but were they past the white water or just resting in a calm pool? He took a breath and began.

'Something is going on in Abdale. You are scared. The unknown can be terrifying if you are not armed to face it. With the right tools, we can surmount anything. In this building. In this book. The Lord has given us the tools. We have his Word. We have our minds. He gave us both that we may face the unknown with faith.

'Consider the story of Jonah. The tale as it is often told is focussed on Jonah, the sinner who is cursed by God. He tries to flee his punishment but can never hide from the Lord. Consider the story again, this time from the eyes of the sailors who took this cursed Jonah on board. Scripture says he "went down to Joppa; and he found a ship going to Tarshish: so he paid the fare thereof, and went down into it, to go with them unto Tarshish from the presence of the Lord." Who were these sailors of Joppa? Merchants, seamen, common folk earning their bread by working with their hands on the sea. Sailing back and forth from Joppa to other ports, days at sea, weeks, months. Some leave at home with a wife and children, then back to the deep. One day they set sail as usual, the holds packed as usual, fare-paying passengers as usual. "But the Lord sent out a great wind into the sea, and there was a mighty tempest in the sea, so that the ship was like to be broken. Then the mariners were afraid, and cried every man unto his god, and cast forth the wares that were in the ship into the sea, to lighten it of them." Waves higher than this roof. Wind roaring like from the very mouth of Lucifer. Every moment death, every moment terror. And why? Not one among the sailors knew. They tried what they could, tipping precious cargo into the sea, but nothing worked. And while they were tipping their fortunes into the brine did they talk to each other, these sailors? Did they gossip and pass rumour, spinning story and story about the cause? Of course, for men are fallible and fear brings error in deluge. But slowly reason breaks through, like a shaft of sunlight through a storm cloud. There must be a cause. Someone must be responsible. Perhaps it is X who is a sinner and Y who is bad luck and Z who is a bad captain? But there is a cause. Everything has a cause. All you have to do is investigate and the cause is unearthed. "Jonah was gone down into the sides of the ship; and he lay, and was fast asleep. So the shipmaster came to him, and said unto him, What meanest thou, O sleeper? arise, call upon thy God, if so be that God will think upon us, that we perish not. And they said every one to his fellow, Come, and let us cast lots, that we may know for whose cause this evil is upon us. So they cast lots, and the lot fell upon Jonah." The captain investigates. The captain discovers the guilty man. The captain heaves Jonah over the side. The storm dissipates, the sea calms, the winds blow true. The sailors return to Joppa alive, wiser, and faithful worshippers of the Lord. Amen.'

As the parishioners filed out he shook their hands, rested a hand on their shoulder and said, 'Fear not, we will uncover our Jonah and cast him over the side.' They departed the kirk heads down, islands of contemplation.

18

BURNETT WAS ON THE ROAD BEFORE the sun. The Very Reverend Reid would have received his letter and Burnett had no intention of frittering time anticipating a reply. They were old colleagues and Reid's house was capacious, there was no reason to deny Burnett a bed. He reached Glentrow in good time, his keen legs powering him down the road. As he waited for the mail coach he went over again the list of people to see and books to consult, a general planning his campaign.

The coach arrived and he mounted, leaving his bags for the lad to deal with. No doubt the coach would sit at the side of the road for an interminable period but the successful completion of another step gave him some small satisfaction. He removed his papers from his satchel and flicked through them. Sitting in the coach he must look the very picture of scholarly wisdom. The Lord who saw all things would see him and approve. He created the world, created man within that world and created science that man might understand this creation. History was the story of progress from the barbarism of the Garden to the pinnacle of Society members. As surely as preaching was the Lord's work, so too was this trip to Edinburgh.

He was broken from these reveries by a voice from outside. He looked up and saw the bushy sideburns and eyebrows of Dawkins, the Sheriff in Glentrow. 'Burnett. Spare me a moment.'

'We are about to leave.'

'No. You are not.' Dawkins had the power to delay the coach. Burnett returned the notebook to the satchel and yielded. Together they stepped from curious ears. 'Off to the capital?' Dawkins said as they walked.

'Some business to attend to.'

'Will you be gone long?'

'I will be back by the Sabbath.'

'I am glad to hear your flock is being well attended.'

'Was there something you wanted?'

Dawkins turned to face Burnett directly. 'I have been getting some odd reports from Jimmy Ross.'

Burnett's instinct was to make a sarcastic comment but Dawkins knew something, or suspected something. 'Regarding?'

'Strange goings on in Abdale. Sightings at night. People out of their homes. Damage to property. House breaking. A false idol. Accusations of witchcraft. A death.'

'Sangster was a very old man, his death was hardly uncanny.'

'No. And the other articles?'

'A pagan artefact was unearthed in the peat. It is an historical curiosity, no more. The incredible accusation of witchcraft was made by the deceased's widow, a known troublemaker. You yourself have had dealings with her in the past, have you not?'

'Indeed. A very colourful woman. And people sneaking around at night?'

'Children making mischief during the lighter nights. Nothing to worry about and certainly nothing to concern the Sheriff's office. Everything in Abdale is easily explicable.'

Dawkins watched him for a moment before saying 'Well, that is good to know. Jimmy Ross must be looking for drama to season his reports. If you assure me that all is well in Abdale, then I am forced to take you at your word.' Over Burnett's shoulder Dawkins nodded to the coachman.

Burnett resumed his seat uneasily. For a moment he contemplated returning home, but dismissed the idea. His sermon would do his work for him. Trust the power of the word. Once his paper was complete it would open doors that had long been shut to him. No steps backwards.

19

IT SHOULD HAVE BEEN PARADISE. A week without him and his birch. Not now though. From the kitchen window she watched Murdoch up on Silma Hill and cried. The village had made its feelings clear. Thursday now, and she hadn't spoken since her father closed the door behind him on Monday morning. There was more than enough food in the house to meet her scant needs and she could live without fresh milk or eggs. Lacking a demanding man to cater for, there was simply no need to leave. After the previous week she was more than half relieved that she could hide from the bitter wind blowing through Abdale. She stood in his study, looked at the books, but boredom and loneliness couldn't make those texts enticing. Was it this science that had made his heart cold? Perhaps it was contagious. If she studied his science, was there not a danger she would become like him? She relocked the door, returned to her own world. It was punishment, torture, solitary confinement. Only so much cleaning and tidying she could do. She had reorganised the pantry. She had cleaned out fireplaces that were already spotless, dusted clean shelves and washed clean clothes. Then she gave in to apathy. She stopped bothering to make herself look presentable. She wore the same apron every day, dirt and water and whatever else had splashed on sinking in. She was marked. Stained. Changing her clothes would give her something to do, but she was drained.

In this state, sat on the kitchen window ledge, Mary Dalziel discovered her.

Fiona registered someone coming through the gap in the hedge and crossing the lawn beneath the washing lines, but the awareness failed to reach deep inside her, skimming off her mind like a stone off water. Even when Mary knocked at the kitchen door, Fiona was so lost in her internal wanderings she didn't respond. Mary noticed Fiona sitting in the window and tapped archly on the glass inches from Fiona's face. The sudden sharpness of it broke the silence and Fiona blinked, rubbed her eyes as if broaching the surface of the loch.

'Wakey wakey,' said Mary. 'Are you going to let me in?' The friendly voice melted the ice and she ran to the door, jerking back the deadbolt and flinging it wide. 'The state of you,' said Mary, giving her a hug. 'When did you last brush your hair?'

'Oh, Mary.'

Mary went outside to collect water, made Fiona wash her face and hands. She nipped upstairs and returned with Fiona's hairbrush. 'Sit down.' Fiona obeyed and Mary began teasing the tugs out of Fiona's long hair. 'I assume you've no news to report,' she said as she worked, 'so I'll do the gossiping. There are all sorts of rumours going around. Strange sightings at night, people or not-people running around in the dark. And eyes. You know Eilidh dreamed of eyes?'

'How is she?'

'Sit still. I've no idea. No one's seen her. Sounds serious. I hear she's gone a bit soft in the head. Worse than usual, I mean.'

'I should—'

'Not a good idea. The old woman has gone even softer. She's going on about Satanic cults, witches' covens, demons, possessions, all kinds. To be honest, you're safest in here away from her. She's pointing the finger in all kinds of directions. After stirring up as much trouble as she can.'

'Me?'

'Not you directly, but that thing your father found. She's obsessed with that. Probably best that he took it away with him.'

Fiona nearly contradicted her, but then stopped. If they thought the idol was here, unprotected, they might come for it. 'So what is going on?'

'This is just the thing, no one knows. Something's going on but no one has an explanation.'

'Apart from the old woman.'

'Exactly. And for every person who thinks she's mad, there's another prepared to believe her.' Were people in Abdale really open to the idea that there were witches among them? 'Listen,' Mary said. 'We've got to be careful.'

'Careful? Why?'

'You've heard the stories about the witch trials back when our grandparents were babies. Once people got the idea of witches into their heads, who was it ended up drowned in the loch or burned by the cross?'

'Who?'

'The young women, that's who.'

'Are we really talking about this? Witches?'

'Some of them are really talking about it. I'm just saying, be careful. All of us. This started with Eilidh, remember?'

'They think she's a witch?'

'Some do, but not the old woman. Obviously, Eilidh being her granddaughter. No, she's saying the witch or witches are controlling her. That she's possessed. They're saying—'

'What?'

'Malcolm heard from Murdoch that he found Eilidh on top of Tiki Rock. Dancing. Naked.'

'No!'

'So he says.'

'I don't believe it.'

'I'm telling you Fiona, you're better off in here alone, away from all that.'

'What else did Murdoch say?'

'That useless lump? He should've been the first one over here, not me. I'm going to give him a piece of my mind when

I see him.'

'It's his family, and my father – I can understand—'

'Don't you dare. Don't you dare forgive him. Whatever that father of yours has done is nothing to do with you, and Murdoch of all people should know that. Every day he's up on that hill. Nothing's stopping him coming down but has he?' Fiona started crying again. 'He's going to get a piece of my mind.' She ran her hand gently over Fiona's now smooth hair. 'And my knee between his legs.'

Fiona laughed, felt so much love for Mary then.

Mary stayed for a couple of hours. After she left her buoyancy hung around but soon the emptiness of the manse, the seclusion the house exuded became stifling, oppressive. She made a light dinner, ate it standing in the kitchen, and then went to bed. It was early, and just beginning to darken.

As she lay in bed she went over recent events, Mary's gossip. It had all seemed so ridiculous during the day but now, with the lengthening shadows, the hoots of owls waking, hunting, the thought of the idol downstairs in the study and no one else in the house. She pulled the blankets tighter. On her back, eyes open, candle still burning. Couldn't sleep. Images capered, pictures of witches and warlocks, Biblical stories of four horsemen, of demons tempting, her father's sermons. Every sound, every creak made her jump, stare around her. She needed comfort.

'Mother?' she said, softly. The voice of her childhood nights. 'Mother, if you can hear me, please protect me. Please look after me and keep me safe. Mother, are you there? Can you hear me?'

Slowly her grip relaxed, her breathing deepened and she fell far into sleep.

20

IT WAS LUCKY JIMMY ROSS DIDN'T give credence to any of this talk of witches and devils. Being out in the woods alone at night would be terrifying for someone who accepted all that supernatural stuff. Not someone like him. A big, grown man. People like him didn't believe that at any moment an evil spirit would rush from the darkness and attack or possess or even murder him. He checked over his shoulder. Yes, lucky they picked a man as brave as Jimmy Ross.

Abdale was a small village but it covered an inconveniently shaped and sized area. Starting at the loch side, the territory he had to cover rose almost step-like past Angus Grant's home and barn to the manse and the kirk. Behind that stood Silma Hill. That line marked the eastern edge of the village. Heading west he went by MacFarlane's inn and a number of homes before reaching the cross, the official centre of Abdale. Here stood his Tollbooth. Beyond that were more homes including the Dalziels' and finally the Sangsters' farm, the western boundary. To the north ran the burn and the old road, to the south, the loch. Eastwards the hills and farmland rolled on to the capital. Westwards, over Ben Morvyn, lay the sea. Patrolling required more up and down than he would have liked, and the woodland between the loch and the western half of the village wasn't the easiest place to walk at night.

He had conceived the idea of staking out a particular spot and waiting for whatever was out there to come to him. But where? Sightings were in all parts of the village. Old McBain had seen something down by the loch, the Dalziels had seen movement by the burn. He had plotted them all on a rough map he had drawn of the village. No pattern, no specific location. So he was back to wandering around.

After a couple of hours fruitless investigating Ross took a break for food. Sitting on the steps of the cross, he unwrapped his fish and potatoes. It was warm enough to sit outside. They would have a good hot summer ahead of them.

He picked the last bone from between his teeth and leant back against the cross. Would it really matter if he went home for a couple of hours and lay down? Anyone out here didn't need supernatural skills to remain unseen by one man in the dark amongst all these buildings, trees and hills. But no, Dawkins wanted daily reports. He stood, stretched, pushed his hat back so it sat high on his crown and continued his circuit.

Passing the manse, something on Silma Hill shimmered. A glitter, a reflection of moonlight, a flicker of flame. He held his breath. Again. Through the hedge in the back he followed the dyke to the top. He slowed down, ducked. This was his chance to solve the mystery, to catch them at it. He snuck up, making sure he was hidden behind one of the standing stones. He listened, heard nothing, crisp silence, hard emptiness. Swallowing, he leapt out.

The circle was empty. He untensed, turned, making sure his eyes were honest. On the ground there were the warm black marks of a recent fire. He sat on the fallen stone and took off his hat, wiped the sweat from his forehead. Running so soon after eating gave him a sharp pain in the chest. Not for the first time he cursed being born so late. Had he been the eldest and not the sixth, he'd have been sleeping comfortably with a wife and children on his farm back in Dunklay.

Again the urge to lie down when a shout reached him from the village, blocked from his sight by the stones and trees. He stood and looked. Fire. Pain or not, he ran. By the time he reached the bottom of Silma Hill he had his excuses ready.

21

WHAT WOKE HER FIRST? THE CANDLE burned out and the darkness sagged heavy. Fiona lay motionless, searching. Sounds emerged. Creaking, clanking. A roar. Voices. Distant, but there. She swung her legs out from under the blankets and pulled the curtains aside. Hell lay before her. Flames leaping into the blackness, the sky red, orange, a sunrise palette exaggerated, a frenzy. She gasped, reeled back, the curtains falling. Shook her head, rubbed her eyes. Cracked the curtains once more. Less nightmarish this time, and she saw what it was. Down the hill in front of the manse, halfway between her and the loch shore, Angus Grant's barn was aflame. She dressed, grabbing at clothes, boots, a bonnet and, pausing only to pick up the bucket from the kitchen, burst out the house and over the grass.

The villagers were already out, Jimmy Ross ordering everyone around and no one listening. Grant's barn and workshop were set back from his house. Silhouettes, young men with blurred outlines, heat hazy and smoke hidden, attacking beams with axes, trying to pull the structure down on itself. A relay from the burn to the barn, full buckets passed up one side, empty down the other, tipping the shallow stream onto the roasting timber, the tools of his trade.

Fiona joined the relay, adding her bucket to the chain. Running, shouting, screaming, black smoke billowing over them and off through the village. Thoughts left her, just the actions, simple panic motivation, the mechanical act, receiving a bucket, passing it on, again, and again. Bucket, swing, hand off, bucket, swing, hand off. Bucket. Swing. Hand off. Bucket. Swing. Hand off.

And the sweat.

And the noise.

And the heat.

It was just her and her muscles, part of a chain, a gang, a line pushing danger. The relay slowed, the gaps between buckets increased. The smoke gone, the fire out.

The sun had come up and she hadn't noticed. Her hands were raw, red, splinters. They gathered in a circle around the blackened remains of Angus's business. The barn gone, the workshop, the timber, the coffins, the chairs, the cabinets. The tools and effects of a carpenter's life, charcoal, blackened, steaming. The smell of heat, the stench of destruction.

Fiona walked dazed through the crowd. She thought Murdoch passed her, face black, streaked, but he was gone. No one stopped. Everyone going somewhere, doing something. She a top spinning, a leaf whipped by the wind. In the early dawn light Abdale was a different world, sounds and smells unusual, uncomfortable. Was this still her home, this land of ash and exhausted bodies?

She found Malcolm wrapping a rag around his forearm, blood and soot mixed on his skin. 'Malcolm, is anyone?' she tried. 'Is Angus?'

'Aye, he's fine.' Nodded towards Angus's house. She went over. A loose group around his doorway, him on the ground, dog tired, arms hanging between his knees. Voices bouncing above him.

'What did he say?'

'Nothing that makes sense.'

'But what did he say?'

'Said he couldn't sleep. Was working in the workshop, working on the new sign for the inn.'

'Candle light? With all that wood? The sawdust? No wonder.'

'No!' he shouted. 'No. I saw them.'

'Saw them? Saw what?'

'How should I know? Well, Angus?'

He shook his head, shivered. Mrs Sangster pushed her way through and sat down next to Angus. Fiona was still outside the main group and no one had taken notice of her. The old woman certainly hadn't seen her. She wondered if she should leave, escape before they saw her, but she wanted to hear what Angus said, see what he had seen. She took a step closer.

'You saw them,' Mrs Sangster said. 'Didn't you?'

He nodded. Her voice calm, commanding.

'And you panicked.'

Another nod.

'And you tried to run. Knocked over the candle.'

Another nod. Quick, sharp.

'Well, Angus,' she said, patting his arm. 'All you lost was your wood. Could have been much worse. You should be thankful of that.' She stood with some help from the crowd.

'Well?' they said. 'What did he see?'

She started to walk away, took a step or two, turned back to them. 'What did he see? You know fine what he saw. What would scare a man like Angus Grant so much he would burn down his own barn trying to get away?' She turned, saw Fiona. 'You know, don't you?'

'The eyes?'

'Aye. She knows. It's in her house as we speak, the source of this.' The old woman walked off, head as high as her curling back would allow. Fiona watched her go, her jerky gait disappearing into MacFarlane's inn. Fiona turned back to the crowd. They stood, silent, staring. Arms crossed. Women and men, friends. Looking.

A nervous laugh. 'You don't believe her, do you?' she said, her voice stronger than she felt. 'That some spirit is haunting this town? You can't believe her.'

No one spoke. Angus stood, took a step, exhaustion

dripping off him. 'I know what I saw,' he said. 'And I saw eyes. Two of them. Gold. Just there, beside me at the workbench.' He shuddered and someone put their hand out to him. He waved it away. 'Now, I don't believe in fairy stories but nor am I a madman or a drunk.' The crowd shook their heads, agreeing with him. 'So you tell me, Miss Burnett, daughter of a father who knows everything. What did I see if it wasn't a demon?'

22

BURNETT LEFT EDINBURGH EARLY IN THE morning. A foul smoke hung in the sky, the streets full of the common sort, cluttering the way, swilling the filth and mire as they trudged through their day. The trip was an unqualified success and he was keen to get home and finish his work on the idol. His sketches and theories had been received with attention, and a well-written paper had a chance of being presented before the Society. Finally, important people were taking notice.

He had spent a pleasant week in the company of the Very Reverend Reid. They had been students together and while Burnett had been above Reid when it came to theology, Reid had been the better politician, cultivating powerful friends. Others were in his debt or in need of his help, thus it was that Reid got a rich parish in the capital and Burnett was out in the sticks dealing with superstition and empty coffers.

His time away, short though it was, regenerated. The bustle of society, intellectual conversation, good food, vintage wines. No mad old women screaming about magic, no parishioners with their petty complaints and nuisance needs.

The night before had been especially satisfying. Reid had organised a reading of a paper by the renowned F. B. Blackwell, on the formation of rock strata. Burnett had held a discussion with Blackwell concerning the question of the age of Creation, raising issues which Blackwell had, in Burnett's opinion, thoroughly failed to answer. After a brief altercation about the process of Creation, Blackwell had left early and in a foul temper, Burnett having got the better of him in debate.

He caught the coach as far as Glentrow and then set out on foot. It was a pleasant day. Eagerness to be back in his study energised his step, spurred him on.

Yes, it had been a successful trip. He had quizzed Reid about potential husbands for Fiona and he had suggested Henry Trent. A young man of lowly background who had made a name for himself first as T. B. Moore's assistant and then as a surveyor on a foreign trip. He had made a modest fortune upon his return, had set himself up and was in the market for a wife. Rich though he may be, none of the established families would countenance such a marriage, but for Burnett it would be ideal: a son-in-law with a fortune, a respected member of the scientific community with a promising future. Reid would introduce the two men.

Old McBain was less communicative than normal on the ferry crossing and this allowed Burnett to view his approach without distractions. Something was wrong. Something was wrong with the Abdale skyline. Something missing. He surveyed the village, top of Silma Hill to the shore, manse to the Sangster's farm, auditing as he went. There. Angus Grant's barn.

'Fire,' was all McBain would say.

As he climbed the hill to the manse he could sense people watching him, eyes behind windows, curtains twitching. The streets were deserted, the gardens, yards, fields all empty. He was brought short by the locked manse and thumped the door. Fiona appeared at the window, peeking from behind the curtains. He thumped again. The lock turned, the deadbolt slid back, the door opened. 'What's the meaning of this?'

'Welcome home, sir.' Fiona was shaking, even more timid than usual. He pushed past her and unlocked his study. Everything as he had left it, the idol safe, his papers undisturbed. He flapped open his satchel, spread his papers on the desk, and opened his knife to sharpen his pencil. Fiona was hovering in the doorway, her eyes bloodshot, the skin around them red and bruised. 'Well?' he said.

'Sir—'

'Out with it.'

In one gush she unloaded the events of the past week, the dreams, the nightly sightings, the fire. Burnett sat down, pressed his fingertips together. Six days he had been gone. Not even. In that short time the old hag had turned the village into a bedlam of superstition and idiocy. 'Eyes and dreams are nonsense, but this fire. What do you know about that?'

'Sir, it started during the night. We were all out with our buckets. It took the night to get it out. Angus Grant said—'

'Yes?'

'He said he was working in his workshop when he saw – the eyes,' she said quickly. 'He said he saw eyes and panicked and knocked over his lamp.'

'Drink, no doubt.'

'Sir—'

'What is it?'

'The village, sir. Everyone. They think—'

She was wringing her hands, unable to stay still. He felt the urge to seize her shoulders, shake her, slap some sense into her. 'I'm waiting.'

'They blame us, sir. They blame you. They blame that.' She pointed at the idol.

'Nonsense.'

'They do!' she almost shouted. 'That's why the door was locked. I've been under siege. They want it burnt.'

He leapt to his feet. 'They've been trying to break into my home? Who has?' Instinctively he reached for the birch. She flinched, backed out of the room. He followed.

'The old woman, about half the village.'

'And what has Jimmy Ross done about this?'

She laughed, humourless. He nodded, his eyes narrow.

'Has Dawkins been in Abdale?'

'Not that I know of, sir. But I haven't been out. They hate

me.' She broke down again and he could get no more sense from her.

Back in his study he swung the birch firm, bringing it down across the desk with a crack like gunfire. He lifted his hat, put away the idol. In his rage, he did not want to smash it. 'Right,' he said. 'Stay here. Lock the door. I'm going to sort this mess out.' As he passed her she grabbed his arm. He stared at her, incredulous.

'Don't leave,' she whispered. 'Don't leave me again.'

'You are no baby. You're old enough to be a wife, so begin acting like one.'

'But sir,' she cried, 'they call me a witch.'

23

MAKING SURE BOTH THE STUDY AND the manse were locked behind him, Burnett crossed the kirkyard intending to get hold of Jimmy Ross. Old Hughie, the gravedigger, was sitting on the wall running a whetstone over the edge of his shovel.

'Ah, Minister,' he said, standing at his approach, 'I heard tell you were back and it's truly great to see you are.'

'And not a moment too soon, Hughie, so I hear.'

'Aye, Minister, it's been terrible since you left us. Madness has gripped Abdale.'

'What can you tell me?'

'Folks are right upended, Minister. Lots of goings on and without you here to explain them, begging your pardon, Old Missus Sangster has been filling the gaps.'

'Do the villagers believe her?'

'Aye, some do, some don't, but most are just afeared. At night uncanny sounds, stepping and scuffling through the streets, through folks' gardens.'

'Have you seen anything?'

'I have that, Minister, just last night. Arose to answer the call of nature, begging your pardon, and as I was standing there taking care of business I heard a splash as of someone stepping into the burn.'

'Did you see who?'

'No, nothing, Minister. I'm ashamed to say I turned tail and returned to my bed.'

'And what's Jimmy Ross been doing about it?'

'Well, Minister, it's like this. My old Ma taught me if you've nothing nice to say about a man, you should keep your mouth shut on the subject.'

'Anything else I should know?'

'Well, Minister, for the same reasons I just gave it would wrong of me to mention the Sangster's daughter.'

'And my own daughter?'

'Ah, now that's a tricky matter. The old woman has got it into her head that the thing Old Man Sangster found in the peat is at the heart of all this and since it's in the manse and young Fiona is in the manse, the old woman put one and one together, as it may be, and came up with an answer.'

'Fiona says she's been accused of witchcraft.'

'Aye, there's many words being bandied about, words that haven't been common since I sat on my own Granny's lap.'

Burnett thought for a moment, shook his head at the whole thing.

'You'll have a plan then, Minister?' said Old Hughie.

'No need of much of a plan. Nip it in the bud before it gets out of hand. A reasoned argument and the fear of Our Lord will bring errant sheep back into the fold.' Hughie looked sceptical but he held his tongue. 'If you hear anything of interest, Hughie, keep me informed.'

'Aye, will do, Minister.'

They parted, Hughie retiring to his wall and shovel. Burnett found Ross asleep on the cot in his office. He slammed the door and kicked Ross where he lay. He woke, hands raised in front of his face.

'Get up.'

'Minister? Is that you?' He rubbed his eyes and yawned, sat up. 'There are nicer ways to bring someone back from their dreams. Particularly someone who's been up all the night.'

'None of those nice ways are suitable for a man like you,' said Burnett. 'And I sincerely doubt you were up all night.'

'I was. Every night this week out on patrol, walking back

and forth through the village. Keeping folks safe.'

'I see you kept Angus Grant's barn safe.'

'Aye, well, there's a story there.'

'There always is.'

'I assume you are here because you want to know what has been going on in your absence? So do you want to hear or not?'

Burnett sat down on the only chair. 'Enlighten me.'

Ross recapped the week's events. 'There is something going on. Someone made a fire up on Silma Hill. The marks are still there if you don't believe me. You can see for yourself. I went up there and the fire started at Angus Grant's place. Which leads me to conclude that whoever we are dealing with is more than one whoever.'

'And where do you stand on the allegations of witchcraft?'

'Well, now we have a problem. As far from likely as it might be, allegations of that seriousness demand that I call in Sheriff Dawkins.'

'With respect,' said Burnett, showing none, 'witchcraft falls under the authority of the Kirk. In Abdale it is I who investigate, I who examine, I who determine and I who judge.'

'Criminal prosecutions are prosecuted by the Sheriff.'

'Nor do we have any evidence of crime. Grant admits to knocking over the candle. As such Dawkins' presence is unnecessary and unwelcome.'

'Unwelcome?'

'What we have here, Ross, is simple hysteria. Madness got up by that Sangster woman. After a sudden death in a small community it is not uncommon. Combined with an accidental fire, the easily led fall prey to women like her. The best medicine, Ross, is a firm hand from authority. Allow everything to return to normal as soon as possible. Bringing Dawkins into Abdale would only stir things up more. Make people believe that the old woman was right after all. Do you see?'

'But what of the sightings? Strange people abroad after

dark? The beer? The bells?'

'Children after playing games, most likely. I tell you, Ross, a firm stance from you and I and this nonsense will stop. You have been too lenient giving credence to these tales.'

'Sheriff Dawkins has been kept informed of everything that's gone on this week.'

'That is fine,' said Burnett. 'That is as it should be. Now all you need to do is write another report saying "The Reverend Burnett has returned and order has been restored." There is no need to trouble the busy Dawkins by making him come all this way for nothing.' Ross nodded slowly. Burnett started to leave then, as if he had suddenly remembered something, spun back. 'Oh and, Ross, I'm sure you are aware that falsely accusing someone of witchcraft is a very serious crime in itself.' Ross nodded again. 'Very well. If I hear that Old Missus Sangster has slandered my family with such baseless accusations one more time, I will demand justice under the law.'

FIRE

1

THE WEEKS UNROLLED. SPRING GREEN THICKENED to summer, saturated the landscape. Heat cascaded across the fields and the crops swelled to meet it. Rain storms off the ocean fattened Loch Abdale and the burn broke its banks.

Work began on rebuilding Angus Grant's barn. Day by day the madness of the late spring faded yet discontent rumbled through the village. Burnett used the pulpit to attack Mrs Sangster in all but name, used his sermons to dismiss the superstitions of the past, to consign the occult to the midden of history. Hearing the same each Sabbath, the villagers took to dozing through the harangue.

Burnett concluded his study of the idol and dispatched his manuscript to the Society, awaited with unconcealed impatience the invitation to present the paper in person. In the interval he embarked on a correspondence with Henry Trent. Trent outlined the reasons for his eligibility. Burnett in turn listed Fiona's accomplishments, highlighting her obedience and experience in housekeeping. Trent requested a likeness but Burnett was in no position to comply. It became clear that the next step would be for the two, Henry and Fiona, to meet. Burnett held back, preferring to combine it with his trip to Edinburgh to appear before the Society, but as the hot summer lingered, Burnett's hand was forced. He had decided to take Fiona to Edinburgh the following week when a letter from Mr Trent arrived announcing that he would be passing through Glentrow on business some three weeks hence and would be in a position to make a diversion to Abdale should such an arrangement be to the Reverend Burnett's convenience.

2

FOR JIMMY ROSS, THINGS HAD NOT returned to normal. People had ceased discussing the sightings and dreams, the presence of strange bodies in houses and gardens, at least in public. Yet the fire on top of Silma Hill and the lost ale had never been explained. Though Angus Grant was loath to openly disagree with Burnett, Ross knew he remained convinced he had witnessed something supernatural.

Dawkins shared Ross's concerns and ordered him out every night, all summer, to walk the streets, paths and fields of Abdale and report back. Whatever had occurred in spring, whether it was infantile pranks or something more sinister, was ongoing. If youngsters, they had yet to grow tired of their games. If spirits, Abdale was haunted still. The storm had receded but the sky was far from clear. A night or two would pass with nothing to report, then he would be frantic from dusk to dawn. Shadows darting behind trees. Branches cracking. A bucket of water thrown across his path. Shimmering light that evaporated when he looked at it directly.

And the dreams. People still reported them, though they asked him for secrecy, for anonymity.

He knew much Burnett never suspected. Young and old, male and female, people were waking in the night to find a set of golden eyes, fiery and fierce, watching them. Mrs McGowan had screamed so loud the neighbours came running. Tam MacFarlane received a deep gash to his head trying to escape. As Ross was patrolling Abdale slumbered fitfully. In this house and that candles burned, people slept in the same room and prayers were said for longer, with increased fervour.

Summer peaked and the crops would soon be plump for harvest. The chill edge in the wind was palpable to Ross as he sat on the cross with his meal. If this endured his health would surely suffer. Dawkins couldn't expect him to patrol all night through snow and bitter winds.

A clanging broke through his reverie. Trotting as fast as a full stomach and tired legs would allow, he rounded Angus Grant's new barn and looked down on the water. Grant himself appeared a moment later and together they glowered into the darkness.

'Old McBain?' said Grant.

'Must be.'

'Not like him.'

'No.'

They ran down to the ferryman. McBain was standing on the jetty beating a metal pail with a stick. He didn't hear them approach and jumped when Grant put a hand on his shoulder. 'What's the matter?' asked Ross, once McBain had put down the pail and they could hear again.

McBain pointed out over the water. His ferry sat a distance from the shore, floating free of any mooring, cut from its cable. 'Ach, did you leave her untethered?' said Grant.

'I never did.'

More people joined them, the clang of the pail audible through unsound sleep. The massed feet awoke others. Soon the village stood along the shore eyeing the liberated boat, assured that McBain had, in his old age, forgotten to tie her up. Murdoch Sangster appeared beside them sporting the donkey-eyed look of the sleepless. 'Give me some rope, a good long bit.'

'I didn't forget to moor her.'

'Aye, fine, rope.'

They found some, tied one end to the jetty. Murdoch pulled off his shirt and boots. 'Careful, lad,' his father said. Close to his ear he whispered something.

'Are you sure?' said Murdoch.

'Aye. Keep an eye out.'

He waded into the water trailing the rope behind him. It was cold, but retained traces of the day's warmth. He kept moving, gritting his teeth before ducking into a swim. The ferry was further away than he had gauged and the wind and current were taking it out towards the sea. He was a strong swimmer but in the dark it was arduous. Already it was far beyond Tiki Rock. He lapsed into treading water.

Ahead of him the ferry burst into flames.

Shielding his eyes from the sudden dazzle, he turned back and swam until he was near enough to wade. They watched the blazing boat sink slowly, reflections of the fire like sprites dancing on the surface. Murdoch caught his father's eye, shook his head. Dougie regarded the pebbles on the ground worn smooth by years of wind and water. She wouldn't have been on board, he thought. Eilidh would be home by now. She always managed to get by them, both in and out of the house. She always came home. He swayed, whirled away from the loch. Behind him, Burnett. They leered at each other.

'I suppose your science has an explanation for this?' Sangster said.

'Which do you think is more likely? That McBain forgot to tie her up or that goblins came out from under the rocks and did it?'

'Like he would have wanted,' exclaimed Old Mrs Sangster. She had watched the whole thing from the top of the hill, her weakening joints delaying her joining the others.

'Mother?' said Mr Sangster. 'Should you not be at home?'

'And miss the show?' she laughed. 'Besides, Shona and Eilidh are there, I'm just getting in the way.' She gave her son a meaningful look. He smiled.

'Like who would have wanted?' said Angus Grant.

'My Rabbie. He always wanted a Viking burial. Shame he wasn't alive to see that. He would have enjoyed it.'

3

THERE WAS NOTHING MORE TO SEE, nothing to do, the crowd faded. Hughie and Tam MacFarlane remained to console McBain, another two or three hesitant to leave, hoping, fearing something else might happen. Murdoch and his father helped the old woman home, Murdoch dripping, drying slowly in the morning wind. His grandmother was proud of him, that it was a Sangster who had acted, a Sangster who had tried to help, even if he had been unsuccessful. Dougie's thoughts were all with his daughter. She was home now, safe again. Nothing they did, every precaution failed. All it took was a blink and she would be gone. Minutes sometimes, hours, all night. Blink. She would be there again.

Eilidh remembered none of it. During the day she dozed, nodded in and out of uncalm sleep. Nervous exhaustion, fear, dreams. She had developed a twitch in her eye, and her arm would flail, jerk like she was a puppet, the strings pulled by some invisible controller.

Mr Sangster was home less, the strain of it, the tension in the house. What could he do? Preparations for the harvest, there were always jobs on a farm, distractions were easy to find.

Maybe his mother was right, maybe they had been cursed.

Once they reached the top of the hill, standing in front of the manse, they let the old woman go home by herself.

'What are your orders for the day?' said Murdoch.

'Are the tools all ready for the harvest?'

'Aye.'

'And the barn ready for the beasts?'

'Aye.'

'The dyke?'

'Done.'

'Right, well it's the peat then.'

'Aye.' Hard, monotonous physical labour was just what he needed. Switch off his thoughts and exhaust his body. Maybe he could get a night's sleep for once. He left his father and cut across the kirkyard, stopping at his grandfather's grave and pulling a few weeds, brushing off some leaves. Steps behind him. Fiona had watched Murdoch swim out, had screamed when the inferno took, had thought him dead. She followed him to the graveside.

Murdoch nodded. Waited.

Finding herself face to face with him after weeks of heartache, she forgot all the questions, all the accusations, all the words that had poured out of her in the night, to the darkness, to her mother's ghost. A minute passed. Another. Finally Murdoch spoke.

'It was never going to be. You know that.'

'I do?'

'Your father would never have allowed it.'

'Well, we'll never know.'

'No.'

Murdoch looked at her one last time then yanked the last thread of hope from her as he vanished round the corner of the kirk. She let a few tears fall, as much from exhaustion and frustration as from loss, tears she had held in while he was there. He didn't deserve to see into her heart any longer. She wiped her eyes and returned to the manse.

Hearing the sound of the front door closing, her father called her into his study. When she entered, he was sat in one of the two armchairs before the fire. He beckoned for her to sit in the other. Fiona had never sat in this room, and she stared askance at the chair, as if it were a trap. Her father seemed, although she knew she must be mistaken, to be almost smiling. She sat slowly, perched on the edge.

'That was an interesting morning. This village is turning into a madhouse.' Her father acting in this manner was the final piece of the proof. 'How is that friend of yours? The Sangster girl.'

'We are no longer friends, sir. Not this whole summer. But I hear tell she is… touched.'

It was Burnett's turn to nod. He already had information on Eilidh's instability, but was curious how his daughter would present the matter. 'You seem sullen.'

'It has been hard.'

'I would imagine,' he said. 'I would imagine, too, that you would appreciate some time away from these people. Away from Abdale. In which case, I will delay no longer in keeping the good news from you. I have found you a husband.'

4

HENRY TRENT WOULD ARRIVE IN ABDALE in a few days and if he was satisfied, the deal was done. She couldn't think in there. On top of Silma Hill, on the ground, back against one of the stones. All energy, all fight gone. Murdoch, Eilidh, the villagers and now this. A twig snapped in her fist. Fix it. Change it. Do something.

Mother.

The swirling breeze danced with the leaves, ruffling her hair, caressing her temple. Her mother watched from Heaven but she couldn't help. The living must solve their own problems. She was on her own with nothing but the hope that Henry Trent was a good man.

Abdale, the morning golden across the loch. Soon she might be leaving these houses, smoke rising from each, the fields of golden wheat stretching like sun rays out from the centre of her world. This time last year she would have cried, screamed, fought anyone who tried to even put the idea in her head. Edinburgh.

'Hope you're casting no spells,' said a voice behind her. She whirled but it was Mary Dalziel, a slant of a smile, her hands raised in mock surrender. She ran to her friend, her last friend, into her arms.

'You're lucky,' Mary declared.

'Lucky?'

'You're getting out.'

'Whether I want to or not.'

'I'd leave in a second if I could. There's something rotten here.'

'Surely you don't believe all that about witchcraft and demons?'

'Something's going on, Fi. It's not all in the old woman's mind. The ferry, Angus Grant's barn, the dreams.'

A tone, a quiver in Mary's voice made Fiona look directly at her. 'Have you had the dream? Seen the eyes.'

A shiver grabbed Mary's body. 'I have.'

'The same as Eilidh?'

'I don't know. It sounds like it but…'

'But Eilidh went mad and you haven't.' Mary nodded. 'Tell me about it.'

'It's… it's horrible, Fi. These evil eyes, horrible gold eyes staring at you, straight into your soul. Wherever you look there they are. You can't escape them. And it's not just me. Many have seen them.'

'But what is it? Whose eyes are they?'

'Who knows. The old woman thinks it's that statue your father has. It did all start at the same time.'

'But it must mean something.'

'Nothing good.' They sat in silence, considering. 'Whatever happens,' Mary said at length, 'at least you have a knight.'

'A knight chosen by my father. That can't be good.'

'Can it be worse?'

5

IN MACFARLANE'S INN MRS SANGSTER SAT with her back to the fire, mug of ale resting in her lap, bones expanding in the heat. Around her, at various tables, standing against the bar or the wall, were her troops. 'It was a sign,' she said to the room, looking each in the eye as she spoke. 'Of what must be done.'

'How do you mean?' said Ethel MacFarlane from behind the bar.

'It is like I said, what we saw was a Viking burial. A burning ship, sinking.'

'How did it catch fire?' said Angus Grant. 'That's what I want to know. Unless someone was on board, I see no way.'

'No natural way,' she said. 'We all saw it. One minute nothing, next second ablaze. The Vikings fired burning arrows into the ship. Did anyone see anything like that?' Shaken heads, mumbled negatives. 'No matter.'

'What have Vikings got to do with anything?' said Malcolm Dalziel.

'Everything.' She sipped her ale, made them wait. 'Vikings ruled this land once. Left their marks here. Tiki Rock. Silma Hill. That idol in the Minister's house. The day my late husband pulled that abomination out the ground, he died, may he rest in peace. Since that day Abdale has been haunted. Hauntings don't start for no reason. Spirits must be chained up before they can be unleashed. Whatever it is wreaking evil amongst us, it was chained up inside that idol.'

'So how do we stop it?' said Ethel MacFarlane.

'Easy. Burn the idol.'

'We burn that thing and everything goes back to normal?' said Malcolm.

'No,' she took another sip, knowing the value of a dramatic pause. 'It will lose much of its power, but it is no longer inside the idol.'

'Where is it?'

'It is being controlled by someone, sent out by someone.'

'Who?'

'We have a witch in Abdale. Does anyone remember what we did to witches?'

6

JIMMY ROSS TOOK OFF HIS BOOTS and rubbed his feet. A new blister crowned his heel and he was tempted to burst it. It had been a cold night, the coldest yet. The wind had a northerly edge to it. The harvest would begin next week. He couldn't help with the harvest all day and patrol at night. Declining to help with the harvest would in one stroke undo all the ties he had made with the community.

A shout from outside and, sighing, he stuck his head out the window. Dougie Sangster.

'Morning,' said Ross.

'Aye, at least you can see that,' said Sangster. 'Did you sleep well?'

He had half a mind to show Sangster his blister, but he knew the farmer wouldn't care. 'What is it?'

'Someone's been at the crops.'

'Been at them? What do you mean?'

'Get your lazy arse out here and see for yourself.' Painfully he pulled his boots on and followed Sangster down the street. 'Were you out last night?'

'Aye.'

'What did you see?'

'Nothing. It was a quiet, cold night.'

'Did you make it as far from your bed as my fields?'

'I came up this way at least five times during the night. I make a course from the Tollbooth up—'

'Aye, fine. So, in those five times you saw and heard

nothing?'

'Nothing.'

'Then how do you explain this?'

They arrived at the field nearest the village. Everything looked as it should. Top heavy crops swaying in the wind, days away from harvest, the dry stone dyke bordering the field and the road rough and pitted all as usual. Sangster waited, arms crossed. There were gaps in the field. The sea of wheat wasn't a calm surface. Holes. The crops would stop, like they had already been harvested, and then begin again further on. He climbed onto the dyke to get a better view.

'What happened?'

'That's what I want to know. You noticed nothing?'

Ross shook his head. 'They have been cut?'

'Flattened, like a herd of cattle's been let loose in there.'

'Is it just this field?'

'All of them, so far as I can tell.'

'And there's no cattle?'

'They are still on the hill, where they should be. And it can't have been beasts.'

'Why not?'

'Come on.'

They went into the field, followed one of the natural passages between the ears, until they came to a flattened area. It was wide, the wheat pushed flat against the ground ending sharply at perfectly cut walls. Ross turned, his eyes following the walls. 'It's circular.'

Sangster nodded. 'There's a gap over there.'

'A passage. Leads to another one like this.'

'What could have done this?'

'Not what. Who.'

'Who?'

'You think beasts wandering would make perfect circles?'

'But why? Who would destroy the wheat?'

'Someone who wants us to go hungry this winter. Because

that's what's going to happen.'

'You can't salvage anything from this?'

'Maybe.'

Ross looked around again, trying to understand what he was seeing. 'We need to go up Ben Morvyn.'

When they returned to the road Murdoch and Malcolm were waiting for them. 'What's going on?' said Murdoch. His father filled him in. Ross's feet were aching, every step an effort, but soon they were high enough up Ben Morvyn to see across the fields, Abdale and the loch.

In every field the crops had been flattened into exact patterns. Sangster was right. Someone had done this deliberately. Each pattern was identical. Three large circles connected in a line by the passage Ross had seen in the field. From the central of the three circles another smaller circle stood at either side. Each field was the same but the orientation in each was different. It was Malcolm who noticed it first.

'They're all pointed at Silma Hill.'

He was right. The lines of circles were aligned like compass points around Silma Hill, like it was the centre of a wheel, spokes radiating outwards.

7

HENRY TRENT HABITUALLY SLEPT WITH BOTH curtains and window fully open and woke every morning with the first light and the morning chorus. His residence in Edinburgh, newly purchased and furnished, was close enough to a main thoroughfare that the sounds of commerce and street society accompanied his stretches and ablutions. In Glentrow the day began at a more acceptable volume. He had stayed overnight at the King's Arms Inn prior to his visit to Abdale.

Trent was the son of a butcher. His passion for scientific investigation was kindled in his father's shop. Slaughtered animals provided an in-depth, hands-on course in anatomy and physiology. Dissecting hearts, rebuilding knee joints, reinflating lungs. When the shop and his family burned to the ground, an orphaned and destitute Henry Trent had lived on the streets, surviving through petty crime and whatever casual employment he could secure. He met T. B. Moore after being sent to fetch the physician, anatomist and gentleman scientist following an incident at Leith docks. Trent seized upon the opportunity to impress Moore and was taken on first as an errand boy, then as an assistant. He had seen out the remainder of his minority with Moore then, with Moore's help, was assigned to a surveying trip into the Arctic. Now returned and enriched, he had set himself up as a gentleman scientist. His first independent investigation was following up a theory whose seeds were sown on that Arctic trip. He was on his way to the western islands to examine rock formations. Eager as he was to reach his destination, the purpose of his visit to Abdale – to secure a wife – was of sufficient import and, hopefully, pleasure, that he saw it not as a delay but as a necessary stop on his journey.

Samuel, Trent's boy, came into the room. Under Trent's tutelage Samuel was learning all aspects of scientific enquiry, from anatomy to physics, ethnology and geometry. He didn't share Trent's love for rocks, but the world was one glorious laboratory.

'Morning,' Trent said.

'Morning, sir. I trust you slept well?'

'Indeed. The quiet streets and fresh air are quite invigorating. How were the servants quarters?'

'Full of gossip, sir.'

'Is that not always so?' Trent remembered well from his own days with Moore.

'Yes, sir. However the gossip here is of an… unusual kind.'

'Unusual? Well, you can regale all the local tattle once we are on the road. Now a good breakfast is uppermost in my thoughts.'

'It is laid downstairs, sir, as you requested. Are you sure you'd rather not eat here?'

'No, downstairs is fine. Pack everything up and I'll meet you at the coach.'

He was shown to his table by the landlady and set to his breakfast with the speed of a man anxious not just to break his fast, but to be quickly on his way. By lunchtime he would have met his prospective bride, Miss Fiona Burnett, and one more rung on his climb from orphan to respectability would be complete. The Reverend Burnett had sent no likeness of her, so Trent was unsure what to expect. He took at face value Burnett's argument that in a rural community like Abdale, finding a painter of sufficient skill was impossible, but a small part of his heart couldn't help but wonder if there was not some other motive at work. Perhaps she was not… ideal?

Mopping up with a piece of bread, Trent felt full and ready for the road when a man appeared next to his table. He saw from the clothes that he was the local Sheriff, and bade him to a seat.

'Forgive me, sir, for disturbing you at breakfast,' he began.

'There's nothing to forgive, sir, for as you can see I have finished. Is there any way in which I can be of service to you?'

'I hope you will forgive my rudeness, but I overheard your boy say you were on your way to Abdale?'

'Indeed, I am. You have an interest in this fact?'

'I do, sir. As you may have reasoned out for yourself I am the Sheriff here and Abdale falls under my jurisdiction. I have of late been receiving increasingly worrying reports from my man there. I was hoping I could impose on you, as a man of obvious intellect, to perform for me a small service.'

'If I can help in any way, I shall. What would you require of me?'

'Nothing more than you would be doing anyway: to keep your eyes and ears open and, when you return through Glentrow, to pass on to me anything of interest.'

So, it's a spy he wants, thought Trent. Well, it contracts me to nothing specific. 'I will return to Glentrow on my way north in a day or two,' he said. 'If anything strikes me as being of interest to a Sheriff, I will apprise you of it. Is there anything specific?'

'It would be unfair, sir, to prejudice your views on anyone in the village before going there. I understand you are to meet with the Reverend Burnett.'

'I congratulate you, sir, you are a well-informed Sheriff.'

'An ill-informed Sheriff is no Sheriff at all, sir.'

'Yes, I will be residing with the Reverend Burnett.'

'Then it would be wrong of me to make my suspicions known to you. It may be they are unfounded.'

'Well, sir,' said Trent, rising, 'if I can be of service, I shall. But now I really must be on the road. When I return to

Glentrow, should I have any intelligence for you, where may you be found?'

'In my capacity as Sheriff, I am forever on the move. I will find you.'

'So be it.'

Trent left Dawkins inside. His suspicions involve the Reverend? Well, I will keep my eyes open for my own enlightenment. It seems I may have stepped into the middle of some local rivalry. Politics, it does get everywhere.

8

THE ROAD FROM GLENTROW TO ABDALE ran east to west along the southern shore of Loch Abdale, following the curve of the water, rising and falling with the undulations of the landscape. Trent had acquired a large coach and pair of horses. In Edinburgh he used it as a symbol of his newly minted status, but in reality he had bought it for trips such as this. He would be returning from the western islands with a large number of heavy samples and needed a practical method of transporting them. Once outside the capital he preferred to ride up front with Samuel, to see new scenery in panorama rather than through the picture-frame windows. Sat next to Samuel, he was also able to learn the gossip his boy had picked up during the night.

'Folks in Glentrow don't have much regard for folks in Abdale, sir.'

'Usual local rivalry?'

'A touch of that, sir. Frankly, they think folks in Abdale are mad. I let it be known that Abdale was your destination and very quickly a discussion was got up between two rival groups. The first arguing that folk in Abdale were soft in the head, uneducated even in the basics of the Good Book, and were open to beliefs that more enlightened peoples long ago dismissed.'

'Such as?'

'The occult, sir. Devils, goblins, selkies and the like. They are of the opinion that Abdale is, in some sense, cursed. It appears that throughout history Abdale has been the focal point of much unnatural goings on. A few generations back, during the witch hunts, Abdale had more accusations, more trials and more burnings than anywhere in Scotland. Folk in Glentrow have a saying, sir, when something unexplained occurs: as odd as Abdale.'

'The Sheriff told me there have been strange rumours coming from Abdale recently.'

'More of the same, sir. Unexplained fires. The ferry was set adrift and burnt in a most mysterious manner. It broke into flames seemingly by itself, sir.'

'Are we not taking the ferry?'

'I have been assured there is a replacement, sir.'

'Ah, good. Anything else?'

'Well, sir, it's hard to believe, but there have been—'

'Yes?'

'Accusations of witchcraft.'

'That is hard to believe.'

'Well I have no first-hand knowledge, but folks in the capital do say that these rural folks are behind the times.'

'Often true, I'm afraid. When I was in the Arctic, we met some tribes who were still existing in savage conditions.'

'You have corresponded with Reverend Burnett, sir. Did he give any hint to any of these rumours?'

'No, nothing. But then, why would he?'

They reached the crossing point and rang the bell. McBain, over on the far side, set off to pick them up. 'That's no ferry,' said Samuel. McBain was in a small rowing boat, all that was left to him after the complete destruction of the ferry.

'Best unpack only the essentials and the valuables,' said Trent. 'We shall have to leave the coach and horses here.' When McBain reached them, he confirmed as much. Samuel loaded Trent's things into the boat. They tethered the horses and pushed off.

Trent attempted to engage McBain in conversation but

received only monosyllables for his efforts. When they reached the northern shore Reverend Burnett was on the jetty waiting for them. From his study window he had been casting impatient glances at the loch all morning and when the coach and pair finally drew up, he had raced out of the manse.

9

DESPITE HER GREAT MISGIVINGS, FIONA LOOKED from her bedroom window upon hearing the clatter of the front door. She had been prepared, in her best clothes with her hair done, since breakfast, waiting. Her emotions pendulumed from deep anxiety – was this how condemned men felt awaiting the gallows? – to excited impatience – perhaps he was a nice young man, a gentleman with good looks and a kind heart. Most of the time she thought about Murdoch and tried not to cry. So when Burnett left the manse, she couldn't restrain from twitching the curtains.

She made out three men coming up the hill. One was her father, another was a boy, maybe fourteen or fifteen, loaded down with bags. The figure in the centre was tall, taller than her father, and his mousy brown hair, where his hat left it exposed, flustered in the wind giving him a young, carefree air. He was well-dressed and as he talked, he gesticulated expansively. She pulled the curtains closed and made her way carefully downstairs. She was wearing a dress she had sewn herself. Her daily clothes were loose, designed for work rather than beauty. She had made this one for a special occasion and was unused to how her body felt in the tight waist and wide skirts. Behind the door she waited for their steps.

Burnett had been very clear about her duties today. She was being presented as a prospective wife, but she was still the housekeeper. Trent's room was prepared, as was one for his servant. Their lunch, a cold chicken spread, was already on the table. Everything that could be done in advance had been. Burnett didn't want Trent's first impression of Fiona to be her running around with dishes and spoons, but one of quiet and composed competence. It took away her safety net: she could no longer escape to the kitchen. Taking deep breaths, aware of her bosom rising and fallen beneath the unfamiliar cut of the dress, tall spine, straight shoulders, chin up.

Steps. Voices. Time.

She opened the door and saw Henry Trent up close for the first time. He bowed and allowed Burnett to introduce him. She smiled and gestured for them to enter. Burnett took Trent immediately into his study, instructing Fiona to show the boy to Trent's room.

'How are you, Miss?' Samuel said as they climbed the stairs.

'Very well, thank you.' Part of her was bursting to question this boy about his master, but she knew she must remain demure. Besides, no doubt anything she said or did would be reported back to Trent.

'This seems a nice wee place,' said Samuel, still intent on conversation. 'We were forced to leave our coach and pair on the southern shore. Do you think they will be safe there?'

'Yes,' Fiona replied. 'Very few people pass this way, so there is little to fear of thieves.'

'I was more worried about fire. I believe the ferry burned and sank in suspicious circumstances?'

'Oh, I see,' she said. 'I would not say suspicious.'

'So the explanation has been discovered? That is gratifying. Was it an accident or something more planned?'

'That is to say, the cause is still unknown, but that fact alone does not make it necessarily suspicious.'

'I'll take your word for it, Miss,' said Samuel, putting Trent's bags down.

'You are to sleep in the room next door,' she said, changing the subject. 'I hope these rooms will do.'

'Indeed, Miss, they are most delightful. However I think my

duty should be to care for our horses.'

'You plan to sleep outdoors?'

'Oh, no, Miss. The seats of the coach make a most comfortable bed. Is there anywhere I could find hay for the horses?'

'I can arrange for some to be delivered to the jetty.' She had no wish to give this boy any chance to meet the Sangsters without an escort. Who knew what stories they might pour in his ear, and the thought of him meeting Murdoch and divulging the reason for Trent's visit set serpents loose in her stomach.

'Thank you very much,' said Samuel, and set to unpacking Trent's bags. Fiona left him to it. Old Hughie was in the kirkyard so she sent him off for the hay.

'Aye,' said Hughie. 'Though I think no one's there.'

'Why not?'

'Something about the crops being damaged.'

'Damaged? All of them?'

'I don't know.'

'See what you can find out.'

'Aye.'

Passing by the closed door of the study, she leaned her ear against the wood, trying to hear something of what was passing between the two men. The thickness of the wood prevented all but mumbles from reaching her. A different noise made her look up and she saw Samuel watching her.

'Do not worry, Miss. If I was in your place, I would do the same. About the hay?'

'I have sent for some. It will be delivered to the jetty as soon as possible.'

'Thank you, Miss. I shall go down there and await it. If Mr Trent should enquire about my whereabouts—'

'I will let him know.'

'You are too kind, Miss.'

10

THEY SAT DOWN TO LUNCH A trio. Burnett had been reluctant to leave the study having someone of near enough equal learning with which to discuss his theories. Trent had shown polite interest in the idol and sat with an expression of thoughtfulness while the Minister read him selected passages from his paper. The idol and the theories would have been of more interest to Samuel, but Trent knew better than to give this voice. Most people saw the boy, not the mind.

Fiona pushed vegetables around her plate, a tightness in her stomach that had little to do with the cut of her dress threatened to return the thin slice of ham she had managed to swallow. Trent's hair was swept back, long enough to catch on his ears. He was by far the most sophisticated person she had met, his boots alone worth more than everything Murdoch had ever called his own. So what was wrong with him? Why did he need to take some country girl when the city was surely full of girls with naturally straight spines and more than one homemade dress? Perhaps Trent had a reputation and ignorance was his hope. Yet he didn't look dissolute. If she followed this man to Edinburgh would she find herself at the dances and dinners of society or would she find herself a skivvy for a wicked sinner? The room was silent. She had tuned out her father's monologue and now she had missed Trent addressing her. She was making herself seem rude, stupid or both. Her father's flashes of anger in her direction constricted her chest, made it hard to breathe. She mumbled something non-committal to

Trent and her father resumed his exegesis.

Unable to get a word in, Trent was the only one who left the table with a full stomach. Burnett was about to lead him back to the study when Trent, who had had enough, sabotaged his plans.

'I wonder, Miss Burnett, if you know where Samuel is?'

Surprised, preparing to clear the table, Fiona was at first adrift. 'He has returned to the coach, sir, to care for the horses.'

'I should take him down some lunch.'

'I can see to that, sir.'

'We can't have you working in the kitchen wearing such a pretty dress,' he said, bowing slightly. 'A dress such as that deserves to be seen, not shut away inside. Perhaps, Reverend Burnett, we could all take a stroll? It would be delightful to see more of Abdale and I can see that Samuel is fed.' Burnett looked like he was going to complain but before he could speak, Trent continued. 'And in truth, sir, I would like to see the spot from which the idol was extracted. I find in my own studies that however beautiful the language used, nothing surpasses standing on the spot and seeing for yourself.'

'Ah,' said Burnett, 'that is an insightful comment. Let us go.'

'Sir,' said Fiona, halting her father in the process of opening the front door. 'If I may, perhaps if you intend visiting the peat bog, Mister Trent might like to avoid getting dirt on his fine clothes.'

Burnett was annoyed at yet another interruption from Fiona, but he saw the sense in this.

'And you'll be coming, too, won't you Miss Burnett?' She looked at her father, reluctantly he nodded assent. 'Then,' said Trent, 'much as that dress becomes you, I think we should wait while you change. It would be a disaster were it to be ruined.'

A new outfit took some thought. She had to look good, good enough for her own confidence, so her father could later make no complaint, but also dress appropriately for traipsing over fields. Once changed she hastily packed up some leftovers for Samuel and, flushed, rejoined them. Her father was waiting in the doorway, his impatience stifling the air. Trent had taken advantage of Burnett's distraction to wandered off and look at the kirk. He found Burnett's simmering temper unpleasant to be around. Together the threesome walked down to the jetty and called McBain. Fiona could feel the village's eyes on them.

'Please deliver this basket over to my boy, have him leave it in the coach, and bring him back,' Trent told him.

McBain, who had been dozing, silently got in his boat and rowed across. While they were waiting for Samuel, Trent saw an opportunity. 'I understand the ferry sank recently,' he said keeping his eyes on the loch. 'It was an old vessel?'

Burnett knew Trent stayed a night in Glentrow and may have heard any number of rumours. He may even have encountered Dawkins.

'Some eight years, I think,' said Fiona when she realised her father wasn't going to answer.

'Not so old for a ship,' said Trent. 'The Encounter, the ship that took me to the Arctic and back was twenty years old and sliced through sheets of ice like a knife through butter.'

'Oh, she was a fine ferry up until that day, sir. She burned, sir, and that was the cause of her sinking.'

'A fire? Well, that makes more sense. Even newly launched ships are vulnerable to the slightest spark. For this reason the utmost care is taken when cooking at sea. Did you know, Miss Burnett, that during bad weather, rough seas or times of action, the galley stoves are put out? During wartime or prolonged periods of high seas seamen can go weeks, sometimes months without respite from cold food, even in the Arctic. I assume there was no galley on the ferry?'

'No, sir,' said Fiona, imagining the hardship of life at sea, imagining Mr Trent on deck in a storm, telescope to his eye. 'The ferry wasn't much of a ship. A platform pulled across by the rope you can still see hanging. The fire is still something of a mystery. What happened was—'

'Here they come, at last,' said Burnett, cutting her off. Behind Trent's back he gave her such a look and raised his hand. Trent was aware of the communication behind his back. It told him more than Fiona's answer would have. Dawkins was right, there was something odd going on, something that Burnett wanted concealed. He had no wish to play spy, but was fuelled by curiosity. He would need some time away from Burnett.

11

AS THEY STROLLED, FIONA SCOUTED FOR villagers. Their route would take them out of Abdale, around the north side of Silma Hill, but there was always the chance of meeting someone. They skirted the foot of Silma Hill and picked their way around the bog. Burnett took the lead, Trent alongside him. Fiona walked with Samuel, and his deliberative pace slowly opened enough of a distance between the two pairs that their conversation couldn't be overheard.

'Abdale seems a peaceful place,' he said.

'Yes, I suppose so.'

'It's not?'

'It is quiet, if that is what you mean. Certainly in comparison with Edinburgh, I would imagine.'

'Have you ever been?'

'No, I have never been out of Abdale.'

'I think you would like it,' he said. 'It is noisy and dirty but there is always something of interest to see. All of humanity congregates in cities. No offence, but I imagine life can be a bit… repetitive here?'

She laughed. 'Abdale can be quite interesting if you stay long enough.'

'I have to admit, I heard some strange rumours in Glentrow regarding Abdale.'

'Oh yes, what did you hear? We are all witches in league with the Devil?'

'Well, frankly, yes. I did hear that. Are you?'

Fiona faced him, scrutinised the playful eyes, the soft face still untouched by a blade. Whatever she said would be relayed to Trent, but of the two men walking in front of her, Trent seemed the more sympathetic. The way Samuel spoke and acted belied a deep loyalty, a respect that was not won of fear. Trent was not one to use a birch to get his way. Dare she consider her future?

Samuel watched her and smiled. She would run a good household for Mr Trent without being overbearing. With a bit of guidance, she would soon be at home in society. Learning to fit in was easy if you had all your wits and all your senses. Fiona gave the impression of an abundance of both.

They reached the spot where the idol was found, Burnett was pointing out features he considered to be of interest while explaining the theory behind the formation of peat bogs. Trent paid scant attention. He faced in such a direction that he could watch Fiona while appearing to be listening to her father. Her demure behaviour and reserved speech were clothes worn at her father's behest. He had seen enough of humanity in the streets and drawing rooms to know the mock from the real. Fiona had fire in her, and intelligence. Was that a blessing or a curse? It was a great pity he couldn't meet the mother. In law, the example of precedent was paramount, but here precedent was lacking. Could he take such a risk as to marry a woman based on nothing but formal responses her father had instilled in her, likely by force? He had to get her alone, or he had to get amongst the villagers. It was bad luck that the bog stood on the same edge as the manse.

He was struggling to think of an excuse to visit the inn when a shout reached them from the top of Silma Hill. They looked up to see Jimmy Ross waving with both arms. 'Minister,' he shouted down, 'could I trouble you for a moment of your time.'

Grumbling under his breath, Burnett led the party up the hill. Fiona trailed behind, stringing the group out into a line. Trent's enthusiasm and curiosity urged him on faster, leading like a pioneer, Burnett next, Samuel's youthful energy quickly closing the gap. There was more than Jimmy Ross at the summit. Perhaps she could feign a twisted ankle and wait for them to return. She looked at a likely rabbit hole for a moment, then stepped over it.

Etiquette demanded that the Minister introduce his guest to the villagers so Trent forced his step in time. At the summit he was presented to a group of twelve villagers including Jimmy Ross, Mr Sangster, Murdoch, Malcolm Dalziel and Angus Grant. Trent attempted to commit each name to memory but there were too many delivered too quickly.

'This looks like a hunting party,' he said, 'only without the means. It is a delightful view.'

'Men like us are far too busy to idly enjoy views,' said Dougie. 'You are in Abdale at your leisure?'

'On business and between business. Business and pleasure,' Trent replied, gesturing at Burnett and Fiona.

'You're a man of the Kirk or a man who scrabbles in the dirt and pulls out nothing a man can eat?'

Trent could see that Mr Sangster's barbs were not aimed at him. 'My business is the ground itself, the composition and history of it. You are, if I may be so bold, a farmer? You know well then that some soils are fertile and others less so, this field good for barley, that better for potatoes, the third good for grazing. My business is the why.'

'And what good does why ever bring you besides a horse and pair and a serving boy?'

'You rotate your crops?'

'Aye.'

'Why?'

'It is good for the land.'

'Exactly so. Knowledge of the land yields more food on your table and more money in your coffers, Mister Sangster. We are fighting the same battle, just with different tools. I notice however that something has happened to your fields.'

He stepped to the edge of the copse and moved attention to the crops flattened, the circular patterns radiating out from Silma Hill. All followed him apart from Murdoch, whose eyes were fixed on Fiona. 'Curious,' said Trent, turning back to Mr Sangster. 'I assume you are at a loss how to explain this?' With a glance he directed Samuel to watch Murdoch.

'I was on patrol all night, sir,' said Jimmy Ross, 'and saw nor heard nothing.'

'A common enough occurrence,' said Burnett.

'May I take it that this is not the first unusual event of late?'

Between Ross, Sangster and Grant they unfolded all the goings on in Abdale from the discovery of the idol and Old Mr Sangster's death to the crop patterns. It took some time as none could agree on the order of events or the interpretation given. Every fact Trent learned was accompanied by shovel-loads of supposition and disagreement. As they spoke he walked around the group, seemingly lost in thought. They followed him, shifting positions as he wove between them. 'Strange indeed,' said Trent. 'I assume some hypotheses have been put forward?'

'Indeed there have,' said Burnett. 'Those on the side of reason and science hypothesise that one or more troublemakers are at work in Abdale and have so far eluded discovery. Others of a more immature understanding of the world believe this to be the work of hobgoblins and pixies.'

'Immature? Now you listen—' Dougie took a step towards Burnett, fists clenched. Trent took advantage of their distraction to move between Fiona and Murdoch and take a sharp step behind Fiona. Trying to follow his path, she spun round after him and lost her footing, the toe of her boot caught in a rabbit hole, pitching forward. Trent moved fastest, caught her around the waist, but Murdoch was a second after, reaching out for her. 'Fiona!' She landed on Trent's chest, hands clasping his arms. Trent glanced at Murdoch's outstretched hands, the look on his face. Fiona too, recovered but still in Trent's embrace, turned to Murdoch. Rage washed through his eyes. 'Business?' he spat at Trent. 'I see what your business is.' He cast his anger on Fiona. 'Your father has decided it's time to sell you into civilisation then? He's here to have your spell cast over him.' He spun without a word and stalked off down the hill.

Oblivious to this tableau, Dougie Sangster and Burnett were spraying each other with spittle and invective. Jimmy Ross put himself between them. 'Reverend Burnett,' he said, formally, 'the destruction of crops is a matter of the utmost seriousness and as such I have this morning reported the entire matter to Sheriff Dawkins in Glentrow.'

Burnett hissed, 'And what exactly did you report?'

'That occult symbols were found cut into each field in Abdale.'

'And as you know full well,' said Angus Grant, 'destruction of crops is one of the most obvious signs of witchcraft.'

Trent moved Fiona apart from the group, letting her rest her sprained ankle by sitting on a fallen rock. 'Thank you for your kindness, Mister Trent. I'm ashamed that you should be spoken to like that and have to witness the squabbles of our little village. It must seem so very quaint and idiotic to you.'

'Not at all. People are the same the world over and quarrels are never unimportant when we ourselves are involved. And the insult that young man gave was to your honour. It is I who should be apologising to you on behalf of my gender.'

'You are very nice to say so, but that's not necessary. Murdoch and I have known each other since childhood. My father is hated and recently that hatred has been gifted to me also.'

'Forgive me but... you and him, you had an understanding?'

'Had, yes. It's over now. A childish thing, nothing more.'

'He doesn't seem as over it as you.'

'Mister Trent, I know why you are here and I realise that, having seen and heard what you have, you will be keen to quit Abdale forever. I am sorry we have wasted your time.'

'You think so little of me?'

'You are a man of society. It does not do for such men to marry witches.'

He laughed. 'You admit that you are a witch?'

'I have been called such. Some stains are hard to shift.'

'I have never in my life mistaken another man's opinion for my own.'

Burnett, Ross and Sangster were still bickering and Samuel was using his body to partially shelter the couple from view. Fiona took in the situation, held her breath, let it out. 'Mister Trent, I know it is not my place to say this, but we may never again have another chance to speak alone. I just want to say… if you were prepared to take me, I would be ready to leave.'

12

IN THE STUDY TRENT SAT IN one of the armchairs, his right leg crossed over his left, while Burnett paced the room. 'A bit rum, wouldn't you say? In this day and age, accusations of witchcraft?'

'Rum? It's lunatic. Who ever heard of such a thing?' Burnett replied.

'When were the last witch trials in these parts?'

'Generations ago. Same as the rest of the country. Oh, I know what they say about us in Glentrow, but there is nothing that has happened here that hasn't happened elsewhere.'

'No, indeed. So, please explain to me Reverend Burnett, what is the next step in a situation such as this? I assume from what the Nightwatchman was saying that the Sheriff will become involved?'

'Yes, damn him,' said Burnett. 'Dawkins will be here in the morning, if he hasn't already departed. It is the excuse he has been looking for.'

'Excuse?'

'Dawkins and I have a history of… well, we have a history, and not a good one. He would love to discredit me publicly.'

'In what way?'

'If it is an accusation of witchcraft, then authority for the investigation lies with me. As if that were not humiliating enough, many of the accusations have been levelled at my own house, so any investigation would necessitate investigating myself. If witchcraft is dismissed and, as I suspect, this is the work of human agency, then Dawkins has overall authority and would try to prove that I have no control over my own parish. Either way, he has an opportunity to embarrass me. As such I hope I can rely on you to keep this tittle-tattle to yourself? Being linked with witchcraft wouldn't—'

'Look good with the Society?'

'No.'

'You have my word.'

Silent for a moment, mulling options. After a while, his thoughts returned to Trent, sitting patiently. 'I have to apologise for all of this. You came here to discuss a different matter of business and now, thanks to the superstitious fancies of a minority of my parish, I have been made to look a fool in front of you.'

'Please, Minister,' said Trent, raising his hands, 'there is nothing to apologise for. I myself must apologise for thrusting myself upon you as visitor at such an ill-opportune time.'

'You are too kind,' said Burnett, 'perhaps we should turn our attention to that matter.'

'Nothing would give me greater pleasure,' said Trent, 'but I feel there is little left to discuss. All relevant details – practical, financial, logistical and so on – were covered in our correspondence, and now that I have met your daughter, and she has met me, all that remains is for a decision to be made.'

'And,' said Burnett, 'has one been reached?'

'It is a serious matter, Reverend Burnett, and one, I am sure you will understand, that I have no wish to be rushed into. Tomorrow morning I will continue on to the western islands as per my plan, and in one month I will return to Abdale on my way to Edinburgh and give you my decision.'

Burnett gripped the armrests, fought the urge to push further. 'If there is anything I can say or do to facilitate your decision making, you have only to ask.'

Trent bowed at the offer and replied, 'You have done everything a host and prospective father-in-law could be reasonably expected to do. The decision for a young man whether to marry or not is a momentous one, I'm sure you will agree. My intention is to think and pray, and discover which outcome Providence has set aside for me.'

'I too will pray and look forward to your return one month hence.'

They shook hands and Trent retired to his room, wishing to rest and change before dinner.

Dinner was a quiet but civilised affair and afterwards Fiona left the men to their science. She put the candle onto the bedstand and pulled the curtains tight, changed into her nightclothes and sat on the edge of her bed brushing the knots out of her hair, brushing the knots out of her mind. One hundred strokes, starting at the left temple and working towards the right, her routine every evening. It allowed her body to relax, her mind to empty. She reached one hundred, continued counting. Downstairs her father was discussing her future with the man who might become her husband. That thought blazed and no amount of brushing would change that. What did she want? Did she want Trent to leave? Did she want to leave with him? Would it be better if she never married and remained here until her father died? Then what? Maybe the next minister would keep her on as a housekeeper.

None of these questions were hers to answer. Downstairs it was being decided and she would acquiesce to the outcome. She returned her brush to its place next to her prayer book, knelt down on the floor with her elbows on the mattress and began to pray.

'Dear Mother, hear my prayers. You watch over me and know what has happened and what is in my heart, more perhaps than I do. Guide me, take my hand and lead me to the right path. I know, miserable sinner that I am, I have no right to expect happiness, but is Mister Trent a man I can give my heart to? You saw reason to marry Father. What was that reason? Guide me, give me a sign that Trent is a good man. Watch over me, protect me, you are all that I have. Amen.'

She got into bed, the blankets heavy, dabbed at her eyes with a handkerchief and turned to blow out the candle. As she pursed her lips to blow, it guttered, by itself, and the room was dark.

13

IN THE MORNING SHE SAW THEM off at the door while Burnett escorted them to the jetty. Trent was quiet but Samuel was impatient to discuss everything they had seen. He looked for an opening. Trent was sealed. Calculating, running counter-hypotheses. As the first few outposts of Glentrow came into sight, Trent spied the man on horseback he had been expecting.

'Morning,' he hailed Dawkins.

'Morning, Mister Trent. Leaving Abdale so soon?'

'As was always my plan, sir. The western islands and their rocks await me.'

'Ah, that is a pity. I am on my way there myself and was hoping to pass an hour or two in your company. Did you by chance visit the MacFarlane inn?'

'I'm afraid not. Time did not permit it.'

'Yesterday was a busy day in Abdale, so I hear.'

'Yes, someone has been at the crops.'

'You saw?'

'I did. People find enjoyment in the strangest ways, Sheriff Dawkins, but in my opinion nothing is more sacred to man than his food and water. It wasn't long ago that a prank like that would lead to the starvation of an entire community.'

'You believe it to be a prank?'

'Well, prank is perhaps not the best word to choose, since prank implies an element of humour, and I have to confess I see little to laugh about here.'

'I was under the impression there was some doubt

concerning the cause of the damage. Was I mistaken?'

'Oh, no, sir. I'm sure you have better information than I do. It is merely my opinion that the damage was done by a person or persons intent on mischief. After all, what other explanation can there be?' He cast his question through the air, hoping to catch something. Dawkins avoided the bait.

'I requested, sir, that should you see or hear anything of interest, you pass it on to me. Can I ask if anything came your way?'

'Nothing you wouldn't already know. The crop damage, the destruction of the ferry and rumours of strange goings on in the nights.'

'Nothing else?'

'Nothing. I spent the day and night with the Reverend Burnett discussing matters of science. Apart from a brief period on a hilltop viewing the damage, the rest of my time was spent in the manse.'

Dawkins could find no way to force more information. 'And the Minister, is he of the same opinion as yourself regarding the crop damage?'

'You will have to ask him. Everyone I met in Abdale, Reverend Burnett included, is worried about the vandalism and what it might mean for the village during the winter months and wishes to reach a solution to the mystery as soon as possible.'

'We all hope that.'

'Then I wish you all the best in your efforts. I'm sorry for delaying you so long this morning with my talk. It is such a lovely area and part of me is loath to leave. Still, I must be off. The road ahead is a long one.'

Manners forbade more. 'Well,' Dawkins said instead, 'thank you for all you have told me. I wonder if you will ever be passing this way again?'

'I intend to be back in about one month, when my studies are done. I will no doubt stop off on my way home to the capital. Until then.' He bowed and Samuel flicked the reins.

Dawkins watched the coach go. The accusations of a gentleman would have carried much more weight than those of a farmer's wife. He gee'd up his horse and continued towards Abdale.

14

AS SOON AS TRENT WAS ON the ferry Burnett marched back to the manse and summoned Fiona. She stood before him in his study.

'You were alone with him yesterday. What did he say?'

'He was somewhat surprised by the talk of the villagers, sir.'

'No doubt. How was his mood?'

'Sir?'

'Was he angry? Patronising? Haughty?'

'He was… nothing, sir. He was a little amused. He didn't seem to give much thought to it, sir.'

'Amused? He was laughing at us?'

'No, sir. He acted like… like it was an interesting diversion but didn't really concern him.'

Burnett examined this concept. Could Trent really have experienced all that and not had any deep response? If he married Fiona, he would take her away and likely never return. What did it matter to him if the Sangsters were lunatics? Trent really was a rational being, able to be truly objective. Like Burnett himself.

'And what did you say?'

'Me, sir? I told him—' she had to think fast. Any innocent comment she gave now could be twisted by her father. 'I told him to pay no mind to the gossip of a small group of troublemakers, sir.'

'Anything else?'

'Nothing of import, sir.'

'Did he mention marriage?'

'No, sir.'

'Did you?' She paused. It was enough. 'What did you say?'

'I said –' Tired, time for honesty. 'I said if he wished to take me away from Abdale, I would be pleased to go.'

Burnett stopped pacing, brought up short by her answer. 'You said that?'

'Yes, sir.' Meek, afraid of his hand.

'You consent to the match?'

She knew the word consent didn't mean 'agree' when he used it. He was asking if she was going to cause trouble or not. Deep breath.

'I do.'

The Minister then did something Fiona had never experienced: he placed his hands on her shoulders, smiled and kissed her forehead.

15

DAWKINS STEPPED OFF THE FERRY AND made straight for the Tollbooth. As usual Ross was asleep, fully dressed. Ross quickly summarised and, since Dawkins had no desire to climb Ben Morvyn or Silma Hill, sketched out the crop patterns.

'Where do we stand?'

'Sir?'

'Suspects?'

'There are two theories, sir. One, the Minister's theory: this is the work of persons, probably children, intent on causing mischief. Two: a large number of the villagers believe this to be the work of supernatural beings, possibly in collusion with elements within the village.'

'So, vandalism or witchcraft.'

'Yes, sir.'

'Where do you stand?'

'Contrary to what false witnesses may claim, I have been patrolling the streets and fields of Abdale since spring, and in all that time I have seen nothing. If these are mere children, as the Minister suggests, then they are more cunning than any I have previously encountered.'

'So you come down on the witchcraft side?'

'Sir,' said Ross, choosing his words carefully. 'Since Burnett's theory seems false, and in the absence of other theories, I find myself allied with that camp.'

'And you say a sizeable number of the village agrees with you?'

'I would say most disagree with the Minister.'

'Fine, that's good enough. Go and assemble everyone you think sympathetic and meet me in the inn. And be quiet about it.'

'Be content, sir. Burnett only leaves the manse to go to the kirk. He takes no part in village life.'

'And his daughter?'

'She has recently fallen out of favour with the villagers.'

'This was not in your report.'

'I did not think it important, sir.'

'Burnett's daughter ostracised by the village? She was on good terms with them before, yes?'

'Yes, sir.'

'What caused the split?'

'Her father, naturally.'

'Who led?'

'It was the Sangsters who took the first steps. Previously she was on very good terms with the family, friends with the daughter, Eilidh—'

'The one turned mad?'

'Yes, sir. And it is rumoured she was romantically linked with the son, Murdoch.'

'Is that so? This is very interesting, Ross, very useful indeed.'

16

ROSS HADN'T BEEN EXAGGERATING.

'Is this the whole village?'

'No, sir. Missing are—'

'Just make a list and give it to me later.'

A murmur of expectation and impatience filtered through the large room. The MacFarlanes were doing a holiday trade. Since they were in the inn, they might as well have a drink. Dawkins let the gossip and chat continue for a moment before he climbed onto his seat and clapped his hands for silence.

'Good people of Abdale, I have called this meeting not to go over things that have already happened. I have been following the situation very closely and I do not wish to waste your precious time or mine repeating things everyone knows. We are here to discuss how to proceed.' A few wanted to speak. Give most people an audience, Dawkins thought, and they will turn themselves inside out. 'According to Mister Ross, my representative in Abdale,' Ross smiled, pleased at the reinforcement of his authority, 'there have been accusations of witchcraft. This is a most serious and unusual charge and as such I wish to deal with it first. Before I can do anything to help the village, I need to fix the legal framework. Are we dealing with human criminals or supernatural beings? The accusation has been made before Mister Ross. I would ask that, if it is a serious charge, it is made again, here, now, before me as the highest legal authority in the area. Does anyone repeat this charge?'

There was a hum in the room, murmurs, heads turning to see who, if any, would speak. No one wished to be the first. It was as Dawkins expected. People were free and easy with accusations when there were no consequences but make them stand by their words and they had nothing to say. He had suspected all along that this would become a criminal investigation. While that lacked the drama and the chance to humiliate Burnett a witch hunt would bring, it would, in many ways, make his life easier. He would be in charge of a criminal investigation, answerable to no one but his superiors in the capital, at liberty to proceed in any way he saw fit.

'Very well, since the accusation has not been repeated, we can consider it to have been withdrawn. That makes this a criminal investigation. I will begin interviewing—'

'I repeat it,' said a voice to Dawkins' left. The old Sangster woman.

'You repeat the accusation?'

'There is witchcraft at work in Abdale. Black magic. I make that accusation.'

'On what basis?'

'All the signs point to it: crops destroyed, mysterious fires, strange creatures moving around after dark and, of course, possession.'

'Possession?' said Dawkins, casting a glance at Ross. That wasn't in his reports.

'Many have seen disembodied eyes, a sure sign of a spirit let loose. Angus Grant saw them before his barn burnt down, half the village has woken in the night to see the eyes staring at them. It is my belief that all these mysterious events can be explained by witches sending spirits out to control the bodies of villagers, and using these bodies to do their evil work.'

'You mean it is villagers running about at night?' said Ross.

'I mean it is their bodies, not their souls.'

'On what do you base this?' said Dawkins.

'Mother, stop,' said Mr Sangster, stepping forward. 'That's

enough.'

'What is enough? Missus Sangster, you were about to speak. On what do you base this theory?'

Mr Sangster got hold of his mother and began pushing her out of the inn. Dawkins leapt down from his chair and got between them and the door.

'Mister Sangster, if your mother has information relevant she must divulge it. If we find later she was keeping anything from the law, it will go very badly with her.'

'Let go of me,' said the old woman. 'She has done nothing wrong. The sooner we find the witch, the sooner I can get my granddaughter back.'

'Your granddaughter?' said Dawkins.

'Yes, little Eilidh saw the eyes. She was the first, only a day or two after my poor Rab died, may he rest in peace, and that cursed idol was pulled from its grave. She saw the eyes and since then she has been possessed. I know what folks say, they say she is mad, but that's not my Eilidh. Something has got inside her and makes her disappear at night.'

'Mother!' Dougie Sangster shouted, but it was too late.

'Eilidh goes out at night?' said Dawkins, looking accusingly at Ross.

'No, her body, controlled by the evil spirit in that idol, sent out by the witch, goes out. It's not Eilidh doing these things, it's the witch.'

'And who is the witch?' said Dawkins.

'Why, it's obvious.'

17

THE SURFACE BROKE, MORE DETAILS CASCADED in, corroborating, clarifying, elucidating. Dawkins had what he wanted: a legal stick with which to beat Burnett. Ross took notes leaving Dawkins free to question. Once they had poured everything circumstantial, everything assumed, everything they'd heard out to him, he ended the meeting.

'Mister Sangster, may I have a word in private with you and your mother.'

Dougie paled, took Mrs Sangster by the arm and pulled her into the corner by the fireplace where Dawkins had withdrawn to. Dawkins picked up the poker and pushed the logs around, focussing the heat where it would do its worst. When he was satisfied with the new wooden pyre he had constructed, he turned to them, still with the poker hanging lightly at his side. He examined each in turn. Mr Sangster had some common sense about him. He had been right, from his point of view, to try and shut his mother up. Few sources of information proved more valuable to a man like Dawkins than a witness blinded by righteousness. 'You have made accusations, Missus Sangster, and they shall be pursued. I will go from this place and confront the Burnetts. But from your testimony it is clear that, however innocent a victim she may be, your granddaughter is also implicated.'

'She has done nothing, she is the victim.' The old woman gripped her son back, a chill in her bones like winter had never brought.

'That may be true but my job is to investigate all sides of a case. Your daughter's testimony will be perhaps the most valuable. My duty is clear. Mister Ross will return with you and then bring Eilidh to the Tollbooth where she will be questioned. If she is innocent, she has nothing to fear. But from what you say, she has information.'

'No,' said Dougie. 'You may question her, I recognise that must be done, but the Tollbooth? That is where the suspected are taken. The guilty. No one has been questioned in the Tollbooth in my lifetime. You can question her at home.'

'Mister Sangster, I would if I could. If everything is as your mother suggests, and the Burnetts are the source of this, then all must be done by the book. In a case like this the Minister has overall authority. You can be sure when I confront him, his first move will be to counter-accuse. I can shut that avenue off now by bringing Eilidh to the Tollbooth. I must give him no reason to cause doubt to be cast on my objectivity.'

'But my wee Eilidh,' said Mrs Sangster, 'she's so weak, so vulnerable. The Tollbooth?' She shivered like a ghost had breathed on her spine. 'I remember people being brought there when I was a lass. The screams. I can hear them still.'

'You are getting melodramatic, Missus Sangster. We are talking about questions, done within the rules of the law. Nothing more. Now, Mister Ross will accompany you, I will go straight to the manse and confront Burnett with this.' He put a cold hand on Dougie's shoulder. 'If all goes right, there is nothing to worry about. If your daughter is innocent, there is no need to fear.' He glanced down at the poker still in his other.

18

JIMMY ROSS STOOD IN THE DOORWAY of the Sangsters' farm. At his belt hung leg and wrist chains meant for the conveyance of prisoners. He had once had call to use them, when Tam MacFarlane's last dog had gone mad, tearing about the village, biting people. The chains had been useful in restraining it before a shovel could be brought to bear on the dog's skull. He fingered them, running his thumb over the locks, slipping his pinkie between the links. Dawkins told him to do everything by the book but surely he didn't mean the chains. Was she a witness or a suspect? The family were through in Eilidh's bedroom. Technically he should be with them but he hung back, a look from Mr Sangster enough to keep him there. He could hear everything that was passing.

'What do you mean, the Tollbooth? What happened?' said Shona.

'She told Dawkins everything,' said Dougie, and Ross could imagine his finger jabbing at her the way it had jabbed at him in the past.

'Everything! Dear Lord, why?'

'He needed to know so he could get those Burnetts.'

'You stupid woman, you have tied them together. That trickster will make it seem like they are in this together. If his daughter is blamed, you can be sure he will find a way to put some of the blame back on Eilidh.'

'But she's innocent.'

'You think that will matter to a man like Burnett?'

'So what do we do?' said Murdoch.

'Nothing we can do,' said Dougie. 'She must go to the Tollbooth. If this old hag had the sense to keep her mouth shut we would still be able to hush this up, but not now. If this goes bad for Eilidh—'

There was no more discussion. Ross listened to their movements, trying to detect anything of concern, but after a moment or two Dougie and Murdoch appeared, behind them Shona leading Eilidh. The old woman trailed in last, her face more haggard than it had previously seemed. Her back arched, like age had caught up with her. She collapsed into her chair and sat motionless.

Dougie pushed Ross back out of the door. 'You won't need those chains. If you lay so much as a finger on her.' Dougie and Murdoch marched by him like guards. Shona held Eilidh in her blanket, an arm round her shoulder. Like Highland refugees, Ross thought, the families caught up in the Jacobite wars trudging south with nothing but their blankets and clothes. He followed them through the village to the cross and into the Tollbooth, the people of Abdale, still together after the meeting, lined the streets. No one spoke. The square set jaws of the men, the misery of the mother. A barrier between them and the village now, alone in their suffering. Up the steps and into the Tollbooth. Ross shut the door on Mr Sangster.

19

DAWKINS MADE HIS WAY TO THE manse forming plans. Before coming to Abdale he had familiarised himself with the statutes regarding witch trials, laws that hadn't been enforced for generations. By officially beginning a witch hunt, he would be handing authority to Burnett, as local representative of the Kirk. The accusation against Fiona made, Burnett would be tainted and prejudiced from the beginning. Either Burnett would have to investigate the charges against his daughter or another minister would be brought in. Dawkins couldn't lose.

With the flat of his hand he banged on the door of the manse. Fiona opened it. 'Sheriff, this is a surprise. I had no idea you were in Abdale.'

'I just this minute arrived.' She was young and pretty, Dawkins thought, not the kind of sallow misery one would expect Burnett to have sired. It was a pity, what would happen to her, but it couldn't be helped. In the name of justice, pity was a luxury.

'Are you here about the crops?' she asked.

'Yes, the damage of crops is a very serious crime.'

'Oh, I know,' she said. 'I hope you find those responsible.'

'I will. Is the Minister here?'

'He is in the kirk. If you would like to come in and take a seat, I will run and get him. You must be tired after travelling from Glentrow.'

'Don't trouble yourself, I shall go over to the kirk.'

'Very well, sir.' She watched him cross the grass, sent a

silent prayer to her mother and looked across the loch as if hoping Trent's coach was waiting.

Dawkins found Burnett in the sacristy. The Sheriff looked pleased with himself, Burnett thought. That was never a good sign.

'I sought you at the manse. Your daughter informed me you were here.'

'I am. You are here on official business.' It wasn't a question. Dawkins would never pay him a social call.

'Is there somewhere we can speak?'

'We can speak here. No one is listening. No one mortal, anyway.'

Dawkins would have preferred to speak in the manse which was, after all, only a house. The kirk was the root of Burnett's authority and that weakened Dawkins' position. Yet he couldn't insist. They sat on a pew a few rows from the front. 'Yes,' he began. 'I am here on official business.'

'The crops?'

'Everything. There has been a formal accusation.'

'Of?'

'Witchcraft.'

Burnett started, surprised to hear the word coming from Dawkins. 'A formal accusation. By who? Missus Sangster?'

'Initially. Others followed.'

'So there is to be a hunt and a trial.'

'Yes.'

'You are aware of the rules governing this?'

'Authority over trial and judgement rests with the church. Punishment is the purview of the state.'

'I judge them, you burn them.'

'Yes.'

'You have all the documents prepared?'

'I do.' Burnett held out his hand. 'There is another matter.'

'What?'

'A suspect has been named.' He watched Burnett closely.

'Who?'

'Your daughter.'

He jumped to his feet. 'Fiona? This is the old woman's doing. It is a lie.'

'It is an official charge. She must be interrogated.'

'I am in charge here.'

'You are prejudiced.'

'If my daughter is involved in any way, she will be punished, but I will not subject her to interrogation based solely on the accusation of a mad old woman who is, herself, prejudiced.'

'Your daughter needs to be questioned.'

'Nobody will be questioned until I have been told everything.'

'Do you refuse to investigate these charges against your family?'

'I refuse to sanction the arrest or interrogation of anyone until I am satisfied with the details of the case.'

'Very well.' Dawkins handed over his packet of notes and reports. 'Read quickly.'

Much of it he knew from overhearing gossip or from news Old Hughie passed onto him, but what confounded him was how developed the alternative theory was. He had assumed no one would give credence to the old woman's mad tales of witches and demons, but it seemed that while he had been using the pulpit to promote rationality, she had been using the streets and the inn to manipulate support. After decades bringing the parish into line, he had allowed it to slide back into chaos. Being a minister was a full time position, he reminded himself, not just for Sundays.

He never forgot a lesson.

'It seems to me that she gave no evidence for her accusation against Fiona.'

'She mentions the idol and Fiona both being in close proximity—'

'The idol is irrelevant, it is a piece of wood, nothing more.'

'Objects were often key in identifying witches.'

'If I go home and burn the idol this minute, do you think everything will instantly return to normal? No, therefore let us move on. We need to study this chronologically. Go back to the source. Now, Old Sangster died—'

'After finding the idol.'

'Yes, thank you, after finding the idol. That night saw the first reported sighting of "golden eyes, floating disembodied." I'm right, that was the first report?'

Dawkins saw where Burnett was headed. 'Yes,' he said. 'That was the first one.'

'And that was –' he checked the report again, 'Eilidh Sangster?'

'Yes.'

'And Missus Sangster today confessed that since then Eilidh has been much changed, so much so that she considers her to have been possessed?'

'Yes.'

'And she further admitted that Eilidh frequently escapes the family home and is known to have been outside on more than one occasion after dark.'

'Yes.'

'Well, I think we can see where our enquires must begin.'

'Eilidh Sangster is in custody.' Dawkins couldn't help a smile at Burnett's reaction. The confusion of a rat seeking a way off a sinking ship and finding every route barred. 'All that remains is to bring your daughter to join her.'

Burnett stood, paced the room, a page of Ross's report crumpled in his hand. 'The Sangster girl is in the Tollbooth?'

'She is.'

'And her family?'

'Nearby, I would imagine.'

'Then it would be unwise to take Fiona there,' he held up a hand the stop Dawkins. 'The next step is to begin questioning, I agree, but you know that Tollbooth. It has only two cells, separated by nothing but bars. If we put the girls together, they may communicate. They will hear the interrogation of the other and change their stories accordingly.' He glanced at Dawkins to see how his argument was being taken. Dawkins kept his face blank, his arms crossed. 'Therefore, since Eilidh is already in the Tollbooth, I suggest we place Fiona under house arrest in the manse. We can lock her in, post a guard if you wish.'

'You agree that Fiona is a suspect and must be arrested and interrogated then?'

'I agree that she has been accused and the law is firm on what must follow.'

20

BACK AT THE MANSE, BURNETT AND Dawkins stood in the doorway. She ran through from the pantry, the fury in his voice. 'You have been placed under house arrest. You will stay here. I am locking the doors and taking the keys with me.'

'Why? What has happened?'

'You have been accused.'

'Where are you going?'

'I will be back later and then we will talk. You will talk.' He pointed a vicious finger at her. Before she could recover or reply, he slammed the door and locked it.

Dawkins.

She went through the house closing windows. A prisoner again, hiding from the village like in spring. The harvest would start next week and every person was expected to turn out and help. She couldn't spend days hidden away. Not again.

She wished Trent hadn't left, that he was still around, a voice and a presence not of Abdale. Upstairs, she set to stripping down and cleaning the room Trent had slept in. Only a few short months since she'd daydreamed of marrying Murdoch, of living with the Sangsters, of having children and dying an old woman, all on the banks of Loch Abdale. Perhaps there were supernatural forces at work, for the world to change so fast?

She lay back on the bed Trent had used, pictured herself in an expensive gown, deep green to bring out her eyes, climbing down from their coach and pair, entering some theatre or concert hall. It was delightful, she thought, a future to dream of. She closed her eyes, exhausted, desiring escape.

21

BURNETT IGNORED THE SCUFFLES OUTSIDE, THE shouts of Mr Sangster, the rantings of his mother. Eilidh was thrown into the cell. She lay where she landed, made no attempt to move. He wondered if she even knew where she was. Putting his foot on her shoulder he rolled her onto her back. Her eyes were glazed, vacant, but she was there. Aware. He knelt down next to her, his face inches from hers.

'I am going to make you confess. The only freedom you have left is to decide when. This can be quick, or slow.' He slapped her across the face, a crack backhand, grabbed her hair and pulled her to her feet, threw her against the wall. Before she could recover, before she could even slide to the ground he was on her, hooking her chains to the wall, spreading her out star-shaped. She gasped, screamed, tears and spit spraying.

'You have one chance. Confess.'

She whimpered.

'You are a witch.'

Shook her head.

'You burned Angus Grant's barn.'

He punched, hard. She screamed.

'You burned the ferry.'

Again.

'You have been sending your spirit out.'

Again.

'You made patterns in the crops.'

He took a step back, punched her hard in the stomach. She

vomited, it ran down her front. The strong smell. He stepped back. She hung there, a scarecrow limp and leaking. 'Eilidh, can you hear me? You're going to speak.'

She screamed, loud, piercing. It took Burnett by surprise and he jumped back. Ross ran.

'Trouble?' said Dawkins.

'Nothing unexpected. You said she is mad.'

'I'm just thinking,' said Dawkins, 'you might have to try a bit harder.'

'I know what I am doing.'

'Do you have the stomach for it?'

Ross returned, pale. 'We are going to have a problem,' he said. 'You had both better come.'

They followed him outside. Most of the village had gathered, Eilidh's screams drawing them. At the front, the Sangsters, their friends close behind. At the sight of Burnett, Dougie Sangster dived, but Ross got between them.

'Let her go!' he yelled. 'You demon, you devil, what are you doing to my daughter?'

'Getting answers,' said Burnett. 'My job.'

'Your job is to find the witch,' shouted old Mrs Sangster, 'and she is sitting safe in the manse. Eilidh is innocent, why don't you torture your own daughter. That is where the answers lie.'

'Ah, Missus Sangster. It seems I owe you an apology. Months ago you suggested there was a witch in Abdale and I dismissed you as a mad woman. It seems you were right after all.'

'I want my daughter,' said Mr Sangster.

'She is no witch,' shouted old Mrs Sangster. 'It is your daughter that is the witch. She possessed her.'

'No, she is not the witch. You should not be too hard on yourself for getting the identity so wrong,' he continued. 'After all, if it were not for you, there would never have been a witch hunt in Abdale.' The truth of this jibe hit her hard, and she fell silent. 'Your granddaughter is at the heart of this, and if she is an innocent victim, she has nothing to fear. But if she is guilty, she will confess.' He turned inside, the shouts of the mob breaking against his back.

'You will disperse,' Dawkins was saying. Burnett closed the door on them, sat in Ross's chair. The threat to him and Fiona was real. Eilidh must confess, no matter what.

22

He worked on Eilidh all evening. She spoke, sure enough, but it was nonsense, useless. Dawkins was right, damn him. It was going to take more than a beating to get what he needed. He had to get through to her. She had to know that no one was coming to save her, that the only way she would survive was to confess, regardless of the truth. It took time to shift reality. He left her chained up, gave orders that no one help her, no one give her so much as a drop of water. He would be back in the morning and by then she would be ready.

No patrol for Ross that night. He had to stay and guard her. There was a chance the Sangsters would try something. He couldn't bear to be in the room with the sobbing, scared girl, so he sat on the steps, his back to the Tollbooth door.

On his way home, Burnett went into the kirk. He needed strength, fire in his soul. There was a time for the Old Testament and a time for the New. This was definitely the former. As he sat, head down, he heard someone else enter. 'Evening, Minister.'

'Evening. Something on your mind, McBain?'

'I heard you'd got the Sangster girl locked up.'

'Aye. What of it?'

'Some information.'

'Well?'

'Some morning months back, I was up before dawn as usual. I went out to the ferry to prepare her for the day. I saw—' He paused. Looked embarrassed.

'Yes?'

'I saw Eilidh Sangster.'

'Where?'

'Dancing on Tiki Rock. With nothing on.'

'Naked? Dancing?'

'Aye.'

'You will swear to this?'

'Aye.'

Confession or not, dancing naked under moonlight was enough to condemn her. Eilidh was a witch now regardless of what else she said. If only McBain had found voice a few hours earlier, Burnett could have been spared his hard evening. He quickly wrote out what McBain had told him, asking questions as they boiled up in his mind.

'What did you do?'

Sheepishly, he replied, 'I watched.'

Dirty old sinner, Burnett thought, but he was in too good a mood to reprimand him. 'And she was alone.'

'I thought so at first.'

'At first?'

'After a few minutes her brother appeared and carried her home.'

'Carried her?'

'He shouted her name a few times but she kept dancing, so he threw a stone at her and she fell off the rock. He caught her, carried her home.'

So, the family knew all this. Very useful. He took McBain over to the manse and poured him a dram which he knocked back in one.

'Health,' he said, and left.

23

WHEN FIONA THREW OPEN THE CURTAINS the next morning, she was unprepared for the crowd that had gathered in front of the manse. She screamed and her father threw open his study door. 'What is it? Why are you making that racket?' She pointed. He shut the door behind him, keeping Fiona inside, and faced the mob. Like ducklings they had followed him home.

'We want her. Bring her out,' shouted Mr Sangster.

'Under whose authority?' Burnett asked.

'You cannot protect her. She is a witch. She needs burning.'

'Your proof? You have none. The witch, if there is one, is in the tollbooth.'

'My daughter is no witch,' said Mr Sangster. 'Any confession she gave was because you were—'

'Extracting a confession? Funny how the two go together. No, Mister Sangster, your daughter has not confessed, not yet. However I have a statement from a witness, willingly given, that your daughter was found, by your son, dancing naked under the moonlight on Tiki Rock. Do you deny this?'

Burnett could almost feel the air crackle, the ground shake under the weight of that one statement. 'You do not deny it. You see,' he said, addressing the rest of the group for the first time, 'there has been much happening on the Sangster farm that has been kept from us while they have attempted to shift the blame onto innocent people like my daughter. Perhaps today we will find some more explanations. It will be interesting to see what Eilidh has to say to all this.'

He returned inside as Dougie Sangster and his mother sank to the grass. The mob broke up, seeds of discord well sown but that information wouldn't hold them for long. He had to get a confession, nothing else would convince the villagers to abandon the Sangsters. Victorious, he turned to find his daughter waiting, a statue of frozen fear.

24

IT WAS ALL SO MUCH WORSE than even the darkest moments of the night had convinced her. 'These things are true,' said Burnett, 'but they are of no concern to you. No one but me can investigate such claims. If you stay in this house, do nothing, say nothing to anyone, then this wave of hysteria will wash over Abdale and leave us untouched. In a month Mister Trent will return, you will be wed and will remove to Edinburgh. Think about that.'

She drifted from room to room, dusting the same spots, arranging and rearranging the few objects adorning the shelves and mantelpieces, then sinking into whatever chair stood near, she sat, lost in caverns of thought. As the afternoon wore on she returned to the kitchen and set to making dinner. She had decided upon roasting a chicken, as that would take time to prepare and cook. She thought to do the potatoes first but found she couldn't concentrate and one potato shifted under the weight of the knife and she sliced through her finger. Holding it tight in her apron until the blood finally thickened, she rattled the kitchen door. The locked door kept her from the last of the live chickens. She rested her forehead against the rough wood. Was this it? Her life now reduced to these four walls. Eilidh's face, the vacant eyes, the bedraggled look came back to her all those months before. The victim. No, she wouldn't allow that. She wanted to cook a chicken and so a chicken was going to get cooked. She did a circuit of the manse, looking out of each window. The village seemed abandoned, not a soul outside. She returned to the kitchen and slid the window up.

The chicken, seemingly aware what had happened to its companions, was reluctant to come and Fiona struggled to hold it. It was a big bird and would, as some consolation for the effort, yield an enormous amount of meat. She got it on the block, in position, and raised the axe, but as she swung it down, the bird made a bid for freedom and, instead of cutting cleanly through the neck, she hacked into the body. Blood spurted over her, soiling her apron and splattering her face. She spat out blood and, rage making a puppet of her, swung again, this time decapitating their dinner. She threw it into her pail and slammed the axe back into the block.

Birling dizzy. She threw the pail into the kitchen and slammed the window hard behind her. Across the back lawn, the trees changing colour. The reds and yellows, the colour of chicken blood, chicken fat. She was saturated with the colours of autumn, the colours of death and decay. She kicked the ground, broke into a run, reaching the peak of Silma Hill in minutes.

25

BURNETT WENT BACK TO THE TOLLBOOTH. He would give her one more chance, but this had to end today. His tools laid out, ready, in full view of Eilidh. Whether she was aware of much, the Lord alone knew. Ross looked sick. The pliers, knives, pokers.

'Ross, make sure that fire is hot. I will be needing it.'

'You are going to start?'

'Not straight away. One more chance seems charitable.'

He slapped her so hard her cheek cannoned off the wall and a tooth flew out.

26

THE SANGSTER'S FARM WAS BEDLAM. DOUGIE and the old woman had returned from the manse in shock, choked at an explanation. Murdoch couldn't believe old McBain had seen them after all. What else had he seen? Did he know what Murdoch had done to himself in the trees? He went out to the barn, took one look at the tools, at the work that needed done, and walked on. He had no energy, he just needed to get away. What could he do for Eilidh? They had spoken to Ross, to Dawkins, even to Burnett. No one was moved. He had considered force, a jailbreak. Even if he succeeded in getting her out the Tollbooth, what then? She was in no position to go on the run and they couldn't go home. She needed to be pardoned, released.

He jogged down the burn road and circled round the back of the kirk. Burnett would be with Eilidh by now, but Fiona would be at home.

No one came to his knock. He peered through the windows. Was she hiding? She must be inside, she was under arrest. He tried the kitchen door but it held firm. Glancing behind him, he pushed at the window. It slid up.

Silence in the manse. A pail lay on its side, a dead chicken half out of it, blood pooled and congealing. He stepped over it, careful not to leave any footprints. He called her name, checked every room upstairs and down, tiptoeing through the house, careful not to touch anything, not to leave a mark. He must be as a ghost drifting through the house. He came to

Burnett's study. As his hand touched the door he felt a fire inside him, a sulphuric burn frizzing along his veins. Some mischief, destroying the room, burning his papers, for a moment he even considered hiding and waiting for him to return, murdering him and fleeing before anyone knew who had done it.

All this had started with his grandfather discovering the wooden idol.

He found it, wrapped in a blanket inside a cabinet.

In the garden, back in the dying light of the real world, the smoke of revenge cleared. The idol was big, too big to hide easily. He couldn't go back through the village. So where? Behind the manse, Silma Hill rose, its grassy sides, its tree-covered summit all good hiding places. It was found by Silma Hill after all, why shouldn't it return there?

27

MURDOCH WAS ALMOST IN THE CENTRE of the circle before he realised Fiona was there. He softly dropped the idol onto the grass behind one of the stones. She was crumpled like laundry, a splash of blood across her.

'What are you doing? You're supposed to be under arrest. What happened to you?'

She looked at the blood. 'The chicken didn't want to be eaten.'

He remembered the chicken on the kitchen floor but said nothing. 'You know what he's doing to Eilidh? And you're out here.'

'You know there's nothing I can do, so don't ask. He doesn't listen to me.'

'Have you tried?'

'You think I want this to happen?'

'It is happening, and it's your father doing it. You have to stop him.'

'My father, for all his faults, didn't start this. Your grandmother did. Breaking into our house, throwing around accusations.' Murdoch blushed, the idol hidden behind the rock. Fiona continued. 'And where were you when the village turned against me?'

'I was with my family. What should I have done?'

'You should have come and seen me. A kind word, even a gentle look. And now you come here and demand that I should stand with you against my father?'

'So you won't help?'

'There is no help I can offer.'

'Then it really is over. You will let my sister die.'

'I cannot stop this. Your grandmother started it. Perhaps she can stop it. If she withdraws her accusation against me, my father might release Eilidh.'

'You bargain for my sister's life?'

'I bargain for my own. If they can arrest her, they can arrest me.'

'Your father would never arrest you.'

'Don't let your grandmother put that to the test. My father didn't start this, but he is a man of the Kirk. He has no choice but to follow the law. You think he wants a witch trial in his parish? He will be a laughing stock in the capital. All those scientists, gentlemen, they will ridicule him for finding a witch. You have to get your grandmother to recant. It is the only way.'

Murdoch nodded. It was hopeless then. The old woman would never give in. He turned to leave. She watched him go. He paused beside one of the stones, looked down, looked back at her. 'You should get home. If they find you out here…' She rose. He was gone. It was all over. Murdoch, Eilidh, her life in the village. Would that Trent came. To see his coach and know she was on her way out of Abdale forever. The village she had grown up in. It seemed strange to her now. Down there, in the Tollbooth, her father was making Eilidh confess to things she had never done. People were blaming her for this, looking for a way to throw her in there alongside Eilidh. They wanted her to burn.

The sky was darkening, summer nights sliding into autumn. Insects chirruped, the hoot of owls hunting. Soft shuffle of leaves. For a second everything seemed fine, the world beautiful. The stench of chicken blood, her face leathery from tears. She walked over to the edge of the circle, saw Murdoch cross the burn road and disappear behind the Tollbooth. Her toe nudged something.

The idol.

She picked it up, half wrapped in its blanket. Deep gold eyes started back at her. Eilidh, the dreams. But these were warm, comforting. She ran her hand over the wood, thumbed the eyes. All of it, from only this. She wrapped it carefully, cradled it in her arms as she made her way home.

28

ROSS WAS PALE. THE STENCH OF vomit and scorched flesh. 'A witch?'

Burnett nodded. 'It is always chronological. The first to see the eyes. The first to go missing.'

'So, it's over?' said Ross.

'We will need to burn her,' said Dawkins.

'That is your job,' said Burnett. 'Mine is done.'

29

DOWN THE SIDE OF THE HILL, by the sleeping cows, darkness coming on, Fiona skirted the field. Ahead of her a terracotta glow warmed the trees and bushes. She was mere steps from safety when a group of villagers with lighted torches met her head on. 'It's her.'

'Fiona Burnett?'

Jimmy Ross. 'What is going on?' she said. 'Is there another fire?'

'Is this the Minister's idea of house arrest?' In the torchlight they looked hideous, gargoyles. 'Why are you out?' said Ross. 'What are you carrying?'

What could she say? That she had been on Silma Hill? That she had been with Murdoch? 'I saw the torches from the window,' pointing at the manse. 'I came out to see what was happening.'

'So why are you walking towards your house and not away from it?'

'I… I was cold, I was going back for my shawl.'

'Look at her apron,' said a voice, Mrs MacFarlane. The white material was dark with dried blood.

'It's chicken's blood. I was preparing dinner.'

'At this hour?'

'This afternoon. I never changed, that's all.'

'Have you seen Mary Dalziel?'

Mary? Oh no. 'No, I haven't seen anyone.'

'And this?' Ross grabbed it from her, opened it. Silence,

then bedlam.

'The idol! Blood and the idol!'

'She's been up Silma Hill casting spells. A witch!'

She thought about running, but where? What would be the point? She was grabbed, shoved between people, ricochet. 'Up Silma Hill,' called Ross. They moved off, Fiona held fast, the idol out of her arms, gone. She fell, tottering unseeing amongst the flaming torches, jostled, picked up, thrown down, hands in her back pushing her along. A blur, a spin.

Mary.

As they climbed the path she had only just taken down, she looked behind her. Most of the village were out, the roads lit up by torches. A fiery dragon snaked its way down to the loch. Malcolm Dalziel called out, 'Over here.'

In the centre of the circle lay a woman's body, lit eerily by the flames.

Malcolm knelt down, rested a hand on the young woman's back. Nothing happened. No movement, no surprise, nothing. He cupped a hand around her shoulder and rolled the body over. Mrs MacFarlane screamed. Rough hands pinned Fiona in place. Dumb, she stared. They all did. Why was Mary out here? And for how long? Ross was pushed forward. He knelt down next to Mary, touched her forehead.

'She is warm,' he said. 'Check her heart, make sure.'

Malcolm did so. 'She's alive.'

Mary screamed. Whether it was the touch, the words or something else, she suddenly woke, sitting up like she'd had a needle stabbed into her. Mrs MacFarlane screamed again, ran back into the safety of the mob. Mary lay back again. Her eyes were open but there was no further sign of life.

'Malcolm. Can you carry her?' said Ross.

Malcolm's face was pale even under the torch light. He nodded, picked up his sister's body, delicate, tender, carried her by Fiona. She wanted to speak, to act, but what, how? Malcolm kept his eyes from hers, his face oaken, his teeth clenched.

'Right, let's take her home, and take this one here to the Tollbooth. She needs to start answering some questions.' Fiona was shoved down the hill, falling ever few steps, pulled up, pushed down again. She tried to get close to Mary, to see her, touch her, help her in some way, let her know she was close, but every time she took a step to the side, they shoved her harder. She bit her tongue, felt the blood mix with dirt, felt it stream down her face and drip, joining the blood on her apron. She swam, trying to keep her head up, her thoughts a jumble.

Where was her father? Why wasn't he there?

One word repeated again and again around her.

Half the mob peeled off with Malcolm to take Mary home, the rest came with Ross and Fiona to his prison, the jeers, spittle landing on her. Fiona was thrown through the cell door, crashed into the far wall, a straw mattress with no more than a few strands of straw remaining, a slit window open to the elements and thick, cold, black metal bars, heard the metallic slam of it behind her. She kept her head down, hid in her arms, and cried.

In the corner, pain and blood, alone. Murdoch took the idol. She was up the hill, with Murdoch, up there in the dark, alone. And Mary? Mary was there? What could she tell them? That she had met Murdoch? If she admitted to that her marriage with Trent would melt into dreams.

Sank on the floor, time passed. People left, went home. Then Ross was gone and she was alone in the dark, the scrabbling of rats, shuffle of insects. Alone.

Not alone. In the next cell. A noise. A movement. Eilidh.

A hand through the bars. In the darkness, in the silence, they held each other and waited.

30

IN LAMPLIGHT SHE SAW EILIDH. The blood. The emptiness in her eyes. Her jaw hung loose, red burns on her chest and arms.

There was a noise. A person standing in front of her. Him. She looked at Eilidh, looked at him. Was he there to help? Was he there to hurt?

'You had both better explain yourselves,' said Burnett.

Dawkins sat back in Ross's chair, folded his arms. Burnett looked at Ross.

'Mary Dalziel went missing. She was missing for a few days after seeing gold eyes in a nightmare, the same as Eilidh Sangster. She ran from her house and hadn't been seen since. Mister Dalziel finally reported it. While you were busy here, I led a search party through Abdale. We found first Fiona Burnett out alone approaching from the direction of Silma Hill, her body and clothes stained by blood, carrying the idol.' He gestured at it on the desk. Burnett made a move for it but Dawkins moved it out of reach.

'This is evidence now.'

'It is wood.' Burnett was dazed. Fiona, out. Blood. His idol. What was she doing with his statue?

Ross continued. 'When questioned she could offer no adequate explanation of her whereabouts and actions. Continuing to look for Mary Dalziel we, the search party, climbed Silma Hill. There we found Mary on the ground.'

'In the centre of the heathen circle,' added Dawkins, speaking for the first time. 'We have a missing girl found passed out in a heathen stone circle, one who has seen visions of disembodied eyes, the same as the confessed witch. An occurrence shared by a man whose barn and workshop, the source of his livelihood burnt to the ground while the witch was roaming the countryside at night. We have the ferry burnt and sunk, we have the crops destroyed. And we have your daughter discovered also roaming wild while apparently under house arrest, covered with blood, carrying the heathen idol. An idol discovered by a man who immediately died. An idol that has been in your house while your daughter was suspected of witchcraft.'

Only hours before, he had broken Eilidh, she had confessed to being a witch and she had named no others. Fiona was safe. But now? Found outside covered in blood, with the idol. He fell into the chair opposite Dawkins.

The Sheriff watched him, watched his brain grapple with the information, formulate it, sift through it. There was a chain of logic at the heart of it. Dawkins was a Sheriff. Making compelling and logical narratives was his business. He knew Burnett would also follow the route in his mind, and Dawkins waited for the right moment. He saw it in the Minister's eyes.

'The solution is very simple,' he said, softly. 'If your daughter is innocent, all she has to do is explain why she was out and covered in blood. You see the problem? Her refusal to explain makes her look guilty.'

Burnett nodded, half his attention on what Dawkins was saying, half on the situation, analysing it, spinning it, trying to see a way out, see a solution.

'But if her story is unbelievable, there must be a trial.'

Burnett's head jerked up. A trial. A witch trial. In his parish. With his daughter.

There it is, thought Dawkins. Hooked. It is in his interest to make her talk. Burnett would do all the work himself. He wondered how far the Minister would go to clear his own name. He was a selfish man but this was his own daughter.

Where was his line? What was his price?

'Leave us,' Burnett said at last. 'I'll get the truth from her.'

Ross started to go. Dawkins stopped him. 'No,' he said. 'We must witness any confession and assess the validity of any mitigating tale.'

'Fiona? I want you to look at me. You have no conception of how serious this is. I need you to speak and I need you to tell the truth. Your life depends on it. Do you understand?'

What he had done to Eilidh. She understood. But she thought of Trent. Of escape.

'Can you explain the blood?'

She coughed. Her father passed her some tea. She drank thirstily, coughed again. 'It is chicken's blood. I was going to make chicken for dinner.'

'All that from a chicken? You have killed hundreds of chickens without making a mess like that.'

'It was… I had heard about Eilidh, I was distracted, I missed the neck.'

'Did anyone see this?' said Dawkins over her father's shoulder.

She shook her head. 'But the chicken should still be in the kitchen. I never cleaned it up.'

'We shall believe her for now,' said Burnett, 'and we can check later. The manse is locked so if what she says is true, it will still be there.' He turned back to his daughter. 'Now, why, when I expressly ordered you not to, did you leave the house?'

'I saw the torches for the search party and came out to see what had happened.'

He looked at Ross who shook his head. 'She was coming up the burn road towards the manse when we found her.'

'I came out to join you but it was cold so I turned back for my shawl.'

'So you came out of the manse and turned down the burn road *away* from us then, realising it was cold, turned back towards us to go home?' said Ross.

'Yes!'

Burnett looked at her for a moment, thinking. Then he reached out and slapped her hard across the face. She crashed to the floor, screaming in pain and surprise. He hauled her back up.

'Did you not hear me say your life hangs on this? And still you lie?'

'I'm not—'

'Why did you have the idol?' He hit her again, she went down again. She lay on the floor in agony, hardness in her. Trent. Escape. If she admitted to being on Silma Hill with Murdoch, her future was over. If she admitted to being where Mary was found, her life would be over. She had to stay silent. Her only way out was silence.

Burnett struck her a few more times, shook her, shouted questions at her, but she'd closed down, shut off. This man, her father, he had never been there to help her. Only Trent could help and he was far away.

'You shall interrogate her? I mean shouldn't we get another Minister? Someone else?' said Ross.

Burnett looked at Dawkins. He had no choice. If he backed out, if he allowed them to replace him even for a moment, he would lose his authority forever. But not now. He wasn't ready. 'I will return home and check her story,' said Burnett. 'We must get the truth out of her.' What was she playing at? All she had to do was speak and it was over. She was deliberately making it worse for him, making him do this, go through this. 'Leave her for today. I will be back tomorrow morning to begin.'

'You are going to wait?' said Dawkins.

'I know what I am doing, and I still have the authority here. A day without food and water, without comfort and hope, a night with the rats, a night with that girl, a vivid reminder of what is coming, all that will make her more talkative.'

Dawkins didn't like it but he nodded. He would prepare himself as well. If Burnett found he had no stomach for his work, Dawkins would be ready to step in.

Burnett took his leave. He glanced one last time at the scraggly, dirty mess on the cell floor, then at the two men. 'I will be back in the morning.'

31

THROUGH THE BARS. EILIDH'S HAND IN hers. No strength in her friend. A tremor. Nothing more.

Fiona ached. Every part of her. Something scuttled across the stones. In the dark, freezing.

In the dark, freezing.

Should she speak?

On Silma Hill with Murdoch.

Reputation, not facts. Folk assume. Folk like to think the worst.

In the dark, freezing.

If she spoke.

Trent.

A whore.

It would be over. He didn't know her. He didn't need to give her the benefit of the doubt.

Trent, in Glentrow, the gossip.

In the dark, freezing. A tremor.

If silence.

A tremor. No strength in her friend. Through the bars.

In the dark, freezing.

Her father. The Minister. Her father.

Eilidh's hand in hers.

Mother had married him. Had she loved him? Had he loved her?

Her father. The Minister. Her father.

In the dark, freezing.

If she spoke.
If silence.
No strength in her friend.
Do I have strength, in the dark, freezing.
Her father. The Minister. Her father.
He had beat her before.
Tortured Eilidh.
A tremor. Her father. The Minister. Her father.
He wouldn't torture her.
In the silence, freezing.
Mother?
Through the bars.
In the silence, freezing.
Silence.
He wouldn't torture me.
He won't torture me.
In the silence, freezing.
Eilidh's hand in hers.

32

ALL NIGHT HE HAD PACED HIS study, the empty house, no supper, no bath. Today it ended. She would talk. She would speak. He had the birch. It had never failed him before. It would not fail him this time. Fiona wasn't mad like the Sangster girl. He would never have to go that far, not with Fiona. She had been raised well, trained well.

'Good morning,' said Dawkins, bright and cheery. Burnett could have swung at him, birched him across his smug face.

'Part of her story checks out. In the kitchen I found a headless chicken, hacked at badly, in a bucket.'

'So the blood did come from a chicken? Well, that changes nothing,' said Dawkins.

'Nothing? It shows she has not been lying completely.'

'Chicken blood? Sounds like a possible sacrifice to me.'

Burnett raised the birch, pointed it at Dawkins. 'I know what you're up to, and you won't succeed.'

'It all hinges on her confession.'

Burnett pushed by him. 'Fiona. On your feet.'

From the floor she eyed him. The birch. A tremor, Eilidh's hand through the bars. He wouldn't torture her. The birch she knew. She knew she could take it. Her future depended on taking the birch. Chicken blood. Came out to see the noise. Returned for shawl. Repeat. Repeat.

'Up.'

She stood.

'Tell me.'

Repeat.
Swish.
Crack.
'You lie.'
Repeat.
Repeat.
Repeat.

'How long does this go on?' Ross asked Dawkins, back in the office. He was nauseous.

'Until she confesses.'

'But what if she is telling the truth?'

'She isn't.'

'But if—'

'It doesn't matter.'

His arm ached, sweat.

'Give me some ale,' he said as he collapsed onto Ross's bed.

'Done?' said Dawkins, smirking.

'Not yet.'

'You are not trying hard enough.'

Burnett stared at him, rubbing his forearm.

'The birch doesn't work.'

'It works.'

'I am just saying, you weren't so reluctant with Eilidh.'

'I know what I am doing.'

'That's what I'm saying.'

Repeat.
Repeat.
Repeat.

'You have failed. The birch doesn't work.'

No reply.

'If you will not do your job, I will. I will have you replaced.

You are corrupted.'

Burnett rubbed his face, his hands, shoulders stiff, hard as rock. He felt sick. Why wouldn't she tell him the truth? Didn't she know what would happen next?

'I am done for today. Let her lie there. Another night in pain and cold, she might be more willing in the morning.'

'And if not?'

Burnett didn't need to answer. He had no choice. 'I'll be back at first light.'

'No, you won't,' said Dawkins.

'What?'

'Tomorrow is the Sabbath, Minister,' he said. 'And you have a service to run. A sermon to give. Or had you forgotten your duties to the Lord?'

He had lost days. 'I meant afterwards.'

'You will do this on the Sabbath?' said Ross.

'This is the Lord's work,' said Dawkins. 'The Sabbath seems ideal. The Lord may rest on the Seventh Day but his servants do not.'

Burnett tensed his arm. The Sheriff stood calm, waiting. It never came. Burnett slipped out.

33

THE DAY BEFORE HIM. AFTER THIS night, the day before him. At the mercy of Providence. He searched for solace in the Good Book, in the Book of Job, the musky smell of the boards, the skin-thin pages, this old copy of an older book he'd had since the seminary. He had used this every Sunday for decades, every wedding, every funeral. Like Job, was God testing his piety? Sounding the depths of his worship? Testing the limits of his heart?

How much, Burnett, can you take?

Give your life to my service.

I will take your wife.

Give your life to my kirk.

I will take your daughter. I will use your hand to do it.

You are my plaything.

No, now was no time to question Providence. Did not the great men suffer torments of the soul, mortifications of the body? How did they respond? By enlightening the world to the Lord's teachings. Let it be so.

On his desk lay the sermon he'd written in preparation for Sunday. He flicked through it, the phrases childish, the arguments facile. Was this the best he could manage? Had age and repetition stilled his talent so? Where was the fire of his youth? He needed stronger weapons. He found the whisky and a glass, poured a big measure. Not a drinker, the liquid burned, but the blaze of it. He threw the papers aside. The idol, gone. The Society in another world. His daughter in the

Tollbooth. He looked at his birch, leant against the sideboard. Please, Fiona, he found himself almost praying, don't do this. Don't make me do this.

Fiona in the cell, the birch, Eilidh's eyes screwed shut, opening in anguish as he seared her flesh. Another sip. A new thought, an old memory. The day he first met his wife, Moira. He was fresh out of the seminary, in the capital visiting Reid at his new parish. Young, confident, marching through the cobbled streets. He saw her first, blonde curls and a green shawl. She was the daughter of a friend of Reid's father. She was there on the Sunday when he watched Reid give his first sermon. He couldn't recall a word his friend said, he had spent the morning finding excuses for glancing over his shoulder.

How Fiona was growing to resemble her. There were times when he would catch her, a movement on the borders of his vision, and it was her, Moira alive again.

Another drink. The burn by his heart.

I cannot do this.

I must.

I cannot.

Another drink.

He sat. The candles burned low. The room darkened, shadows climbing down from bookshelves, crawling across the floor like the spectres of damned souls inching their way to him. He sat, his head drooping, his hand sliding off the glass onto the desk. He fell forward, hard asleep on the wine-dark desk.

In the darkness, eyes.

34

HE PREPARED HIMSELF, MADE HIS WAY to the kirk.

The congregation gathered. From the vestry he watched them file in. This was the first time he had seen the villagers since his daughter had been accused and arrested. He knew them, knew their pettiness, knew the hatred they held in their hearts. They weren't coming to learn today, they were coming to gawp. Well, he was ready for them. He knew what to say and he knew what to do. His authority was paramount. And what did simple folk love more than an evildoer? A righteous victim.

He stepped out to the altar and began. The ritual was his friend, tradition on his side. None could gainsay the church, none dared interrupt a service. They stood, they knelt, they prayed, they sang, all when he commanded it, the kirk much quieter than usual. Everyone had reason to pray this week, those who still came. In this building he was God's man. This was his house.

Time for the reading. He looked out over the congregation. Which were his enemies? he wondered. Which could he rely on? It would begin now.

He read: 'And it came to pass after these things, that God did tempt Abraham, and said unto him, Abraham: and he said, Behold, here I am. And he said, Take now thy son, thine only son Isaac, whom thou lovest, and get thee into the land of Moriah; and offer him there for a burnt offering upon one of the mountains which I will tell thee of.

'And Abraham rose up early in the morning, and saddled

his ass, and took two of his young men with him, and Isaac his son, and clave the wood for the burnt offering, and rose up, and went unto the place of which God had told him.

'Then on the third day Abraham lifted up his eyes, and saw the place afar off.

'And Abraham said unto his young men, Abide ye here with the ass; and I and the lad will go yonder and worship, and come again to you.

'And Abraham took the wood of the burnt offering, and laid it upon Isaac his son; and he took the fire in his hand, and a knife; and they went both of them together.

'And Isaac spake unto Abraham his father, and said, My father: and he said, Here am I, my son. And he said, Behold the fire and the wood: but where is the lamb for a burnt offering?

'And Abraham said, My son, God will provide himself a lamb for a burnt offering: so they went both of them together.

'And they came to the place which God had told him of; and Abraham built an altar there, and laid the wood in order, and bound Isaac his son, and laid him on the altar upon the wood.

'And Abraham stretched forth his hand, and took the knife to slay his son.

'And the angel of the Lord called unto him out of heaven, and said, Abraham, Abraham: and he said, Here am I. And he said, Lay not thine hand upon the lad, neither do thou any thing unto him: for now I know that thou fearest God, seeing thou hast not withheld thy son, thine only son from me.

'And Abraham lifted up his eyes, and looked, and behold behind him a ram caught in a thicket by his horns: and Abraham went and took the ram, and offered him up for a burnt offering in the stead of his son.'

As he climbed down and Psalm 116 began, he cast a quick glance at Dawkins. He had a smile upturning the edge of his mouth. So, he knows what I am up to, thought Burnett. Well, that is to be expected. This will be done by the book. He will have no way to fault me, and I will get my way in the end.

'Psalm 116 asks us *What shall I render unto the Lord?*' He paused, looked sternly across the nave. '*What* shall I render unto the Lord? What shall *I* render unto the Lord. What would you render unto the Lord?'

He spoke slowly, quietly. The congregation had to lean forward for every word. The delivery, he knew, would unsettle them. He was a fire and brimstone preacher, delivering dire warnings and harsh truths from this pulpit week in week out for more than three decades.

'We meet the Lord naked and exposed, our souls bared, our every deed lying before Him. What have we to offer him? What shall I render unto Him?'

A pause, long and weighty.

'Abraham was prepared to render his only begotten son unto the Lord. That is faith. That is true faith. A son for a son.'

His eyes fell on Christ crucified. The pained face, the wounds, the blood.

'A son for a son. What shall *I* render unto the Lord?'

He brought has hand down sharply, the crack echoing through the chill stones of the kirk.

'An evil walks through Abdale. Some of you pretend at knowledge, call it names vaguely remembered from childhood nightmares. One of our daughters has confessed. Another is afflicted. A third is blamed. A fire. Dreams. What shall I render unto the Lord? Evil has many names. There are many evils. We do not as yet know which evil has been visited upon us. We do not as yet know why. Are we, like Abraham, being tested? Are we, like Job, being tormented? Are we, like Jonah, being punished?'

He leant forward, face stern.

'For be assured, whether it is a test, a torment or a punishment, it is meant for us all. This is Abdale's burden. Every one of you has sin in your heart. Every one of you has secrets. Every one of you has need to worry about his immortal soul. Not one of you is guaranteed a place in Paradise. Not one of you, and me neither. He died for us sinners, a son for a son. And our thanks has been pitiful. What shall I render unto the Lord?'

He straightened up again.

'One has confessed. Another is accused. As Minister of this parish I have a duty to find the truth by all and any means at my disposal. This I undertake. It is my test. My torment. My punishment. And I will see it through. I shall render everything unto the Lord.'

A pause. A long, empty pause.

'And you?' he said, finally. 'Each single one of you. What shall you render unto the Lord? He knows. He watches. He hears. He is with us now, in the kirk, in our hearts, in our souls. What shall *you* render unto Him?'

35

WITH CONFIDENCE HE MARCHED INTO THE cell, Jimmy Ross trailing him, Dawkins following at his own pace. Villagers stood outside clumped in groups, keeping their distance, close enough for news to spread fast. Eilidh's confession, Mary's discovery, Fiona's arrest. There were no secrets anymore. No gossip. It was true, a witch in the village. And old Mrs Sangster's granddaughter, well that made sense, when you thought about it. They had gathered to see what came next.

Murdoch sat slumped under the cross. Should he speak? Tell them Fiona had been with him. Would it free her? Would they clap him in irons? She hadn't named him. Ross hadn't come for him. Why hadn't she named him? Was it her honour? A young man could do what he liked in the woods, that was looked upon with understanding, but not a young girl. Would she go through torture to save her reputation?

Burnett ordered the cell open. Dawkins leaned back in the chair, reclining to watch the show. Burnett flexed the birch and stepped into the cell.

Fiona knew little but thirst and hunger. Her body ached, ankles and wrists from the chains, her skin aflame from the birch, wounds trying to seal torn open with every twitch as she tried to find light, to make sense of where she was, what was going on. The noise of the door, the step of hard boots. It was him.

'Fiona? Fiona can you hear me?'

She scuttled back from him, tried to push herself into the

wall.

'Now, this is very simple. You will tell me the reason for your being out of the house when they arrested you.'

A shaken head, hair dancing over her face.

'You will tell me.'

He put the rod in the fire. More scuttling against the wall. Over his shoulder he could feel Dawkins watching. 'Look at me, girl.'

She coughed, her throat glued dry.

'Have you fed her? Given her water?'

Ross shook his head.

She coughed again.

'Fiona. Can you hear me? Fiona, you have to tell me. Why were you out of the house?'

Nothing.

'You have to tell us. Please. Speak.'

She shook her hair, screwed up her eyes. Can't say. Can't say. The punishment, he'd beat her, thrash her, throw her out, her life over, a harlot, a whore, a sinner.

'Fiona! You must speak. I command it.'

She caught her voice. 'No!'

'Fiona! This is your father. Where were you?'

She laughed, an animalistic bark.

'Why were you outside?'

'No! No! No! No! No!'

And he slapped her, short and fierce. She stopped. Looked straight at him, deep in the eyes. He felt something, a coldness, a fear. They moved back from each other. She curled up in the corner. He stepped out of the cell.

'Well?' said Dawkins.

'A day hasn't done any good.'

'Do you think she is under demonic control?'

Burnett paused. There was no safe way to answer. Yes and the Devil was in her, she had done the things she had been accused of. No and she was the one doing the controlling. 'If there is no confession, I will order a trial convened.'

Burnett could only nod. Dawkins smiled.

The tools were ready, the fire hot. It was time.

'Father, no!'

Again. Again. Eyes on him, watching. Any flinch, any lessening of his will and he'd be as guilty as she. Again. Again.

'Mother! Help me!'

Burnt flesh. What had she said? Behind him he heard Dawkins and Ross.

'Mother?'

'Dead, sir.'

'And she calls to her? Interesting.'

'You will speak, girl.'

The pain, such pain. Her mind went white. Red. Gold.

He stood, pliers gripped, her fingernail held firm in them. Nausea. A memory, her mother sitting next to an empty crib, belly large with child. He shook his head.

'Will you speak now?'

'Mother!'

On the third nail he ripped flesh, stripped skin from her digit. The scream stopped him dead, another memory, his wife in childbirth, the same scream.

He dropped the pliers, knelt beside her.

'For God's sake girl, speak. Tell me what you were doing?'

She choked, coughed up blood. She had bitten hard on her tongue.

'I—'

'Yes?'

Dawkins and Ross were outside the cell, ready.

'Silma Hill.'

'She admits it,' said Dawkins. 'In the circle, casting spells. Where we found Mary.'

'No!' she screamed. 'No, not Mary.'

Dawkins picked up the pliers, took a step into the cell. Burnett held up his hand. Placed it on Fiona's head.

'Speak, and it will be done.'

'Murdoch. I was with Murdoch.'

'With… with Murdoch? Murdoch Sangster?'

'The brother of the witch,' Ross explained to Dawkins.

'You were up Silma Hill with Murdoch Sangster?'

'We spoke. Only spoke. He left. I came home and they found me.'

'You lay with him?' He felt light-headed, put his hand out to steady himself. His daughter, lying with a man. His reputation was ruined. The father of a slattern, the minister whose daughter freely gave herself to others.

'No!'

A shaft of light. 'Rape!'

'No! Nothing happened.'

'This is nonsense,' said Dawkins. 'We have a confession that Eilidh is a witch. At the same time this one admits to being on top of the hill with the witch's brother after which we find a girl close to death. She was covered in blood.'

She was beyond his help. He couldn't salvage anything from this but himself. He turned, rage burning.

'Get the boy.'

36

ANOTHER CONFESSION. A SECOND WITCH. AND a name. Someone named. Ross was coming, armed. Everyone stepped back, all but one. Alone by the cross he waited for Ross, let him clap the irons on, let himself be led inside.

Fiona on the floor. He saw the blood, the ripped fingers. He saw Eilidh hanging limp from the wall. Was she even alive? His body emptied, his spirit fled.

'You have been named,' said Dawkins.

'Yes.'

'Do you deny it?'

'No.'

'You lay with my daughter.'

'No.'

'So you do deny it.'

'We were in love. We wished to marry. But that is long over. My sister; what you did. We did nothing but talk. Her honour is pure. I left while it was still light. After that I don't know what happened.'

'And Mary Dalziel. What of her?'

'I know nothing of that.'

'Your sister is a witch. Your lover is a witch,' said Dawkins. 'You were with her in the stone circle. I put it to you that you were engaged in Satanic rites. I put it to you that you are a witch.'

He didn't answer.

'We can make you talk.'

Murdoch raised his head. Looked at Burnett. 'I know how this works. I am no fool. You have two confessions, one naming me. I am already guilty. I confess. I am a witch. Burn me. Do what you like. I no longer care. All I cared for lies bleeding in that cell. I know you will burn your own daughter, sir. Well, burn me with her.'

WATER

1

THE DELUGE MADE THE ROAD ALONG Loch Abdale from Glentrow too dangerous that late in the day. Rain swirling, drilling from all angles. For Samuel, raising his head was an endurance, watching the road a Sisyphean task. Fortunately, there were plenty of rooms at the King's Arms Inn. Few travellers came this way after harvest. While Samuel saw to the horses' stabling, Trent stood with his back to the roaring fire, drying himself with the brandy Mrs Collins, the landlady, had furnished him. The blood flowing again and his britches retaining more heat than was comfortable, he moved to one of the four armchairs arrayed in a semi-circle around the grate. The door opened and three men entered. They went straight for the fire while their servants dealt with the landlady.

Wrapped in layers, Trent could make out little of their appearance. Two of the men were old, their whiskers already grey and their skins a ruddy red which Trent suspected was more in keeping with a lifetime of healthy drinking than their recent exposure to the elements. The third was younger, about Trent's age. They were officials of some kind, the two older men suffused with the confidence of men used to being obeyed, the younger carrying himself with the bearing of one in expectation of a future. He nodded at Trent and took up his position beside his colleagues, attempting to manoeuvre some part of his body towards the heat. Their bulk blocked all warmth from reaching Trent.

Defrosting, they began to pay attention to their surroundings and noticed Trent, or, more accurately, noticed his brandy. One of the older made a sign to his servant and momentarily three brandies appeared. The other older man started slightly. Trent turned his attention to this man who began to unwrap his muffler and reveal his face. Trent was astounded to see before him the Very Reverend Reid.

'Trent! What the Devil are you doing here? I thought you were out in the wilds collecting rocks.'

'Sir, what a pleasure to meet you here. For myself, I am on my way back to Edinburgh, but I never expected to meet you so far from home.'

'Gentlemen,' said Reid, 'this is Mister Henry Trent, a friend of mine and a scientist of some note.' Trent bowed at the compliment and then in turn at the two other men as Reid introduced them. 'This surly fellow is Sir Robert Dalrymple and this young chap is Mister James Harrison, a lawyer and clerk in the Justice's office.'

'Sir Robert, your reputation precedes you. It is an honour to meet you.'

Sir Robert nodded acknowledgement. Trent shook hands with Harrison and, formalities complete, each man sank into an armchair.

'So, if I may be so bold,' began Trent, 'what brings such distinguished men as yourselves to Glentrow on a bitter winter day?'

'That damn fool Burnett,' said Reid. 'Have you heard what he has done?'

'Burnett?'

'Ah yes, I forgot, you were to pay him a visit regarding the hand of his daughter. Did you?'

'I did and it was my intention to return there tomorrow. Has something happened?'

'When were you there?' Reid continued.

'A month ago, for one night only.'

'Did anything strike you as unusual at the time?'

Trent wondered what had happened in the meantime, and decided complete openness was the only tactic. 'There had been some strange events before I arrived. A number of fires, including one which sank the ferry, and the day I arrived the crops had been vandalised, occult patterns made amongst the fields.'

'Did Burnett offer any explanation at the time?'

'His theory was mischief, children most probably.'

'Did you hear any other theories?'

Trent hesitated, then continued. 'Yes, some of the villagers spoke of witchcraft.'

Sir Robert harrumphed. 'Have you heard anything from Abdale since that time?' said Reid.

'No, sir. I've been on the western islands and just arrived in Glentrow shortly before you gentlemen. It was my intention to continue to Abdale today, where I am expected, but the weather, as you know—'

'You are expected? By Burnett?'

'Around this time, yes. The matter which previously took me to Abdale remains to be concluded. I promised to return in a month on my way home. Thus, I am here.'

'You have decided?' Trent had no wish to discuss his private matter in public, so merely nodded an affirmative. 'I wouldn't be too hasty,' said Reid.

'May I ask, sir, what you mean by that?'

'Burnett has instigated a witch hunt.'

'A witch hunt? He took them seriously?'

'As far as we can ascertain he was forced into it by circumstance and by the local Sheriff.'

'Dawkins?'

'You know him?'

'I met him in this very inn. He asked me to act as a spy for him in Abdale.'

'Did you?' said Sir Robert, speaking for the first time.

'I found out nothing he did not already know.' Trent shook

his head. An actual witch hunt. 'Do you know, sir, if the Reverend Burnett has—'

'Found any real witches?' Reid laughed. 'This is as ludicrous to us as it is to you, Trent. Has he found any?' He looked at Sir Robert, who made a sign to Harrison.

The clerk handed Trent some papers. 'That's Dawkins' latest report,' he said.

Trent read, exclaiming when he reached the tallies. He read snatches aloud: 'To date, nine confessions of witchcraft. The Tollbooth full to overflow. Request permission to carry out sentences.'

'Burning,' said Harrison.

'I find all of this hard to believe, sir. I mean, witches in Abdale? Witches anywhere?'

'No doubt the confessions were not made freely, but if confessions were made, we are in a quandary,' said Reid.

'How so?'

'As much as we may dismiss these superstitions of the past, they remain crimes and as such must be punished.'

'You go to Abdale in the morning?' asked Trent.

'We do.'

'Might I be permitted to travel with you?'

'You still plan to go?'

'Of course.'

'One of the guilty. One of the confessed witches—'

'Yes?'

'Is Burnett's daughter.'

'Fiona? Confessed?'

'She did.'

'Freely?'

'We don't know.'

'So either—'

'Either she freely confessed to being a witch or her father interrogated her until she confessed.'

'Interrogated. Tortured.'

'Yes.'

'And you still wish to come?'

Trent didn't answer. His month in the wild of the western islands had clarified little. Each night he sat by the fire with a glass much like this, and, like his father had with cuts of beef, he weighed and balanced, trimmed and filleted. Was this really how the most serious of decisions were made? A single meeting. A future based on appearance and instinct. But his word had been given, a month had passed and he must reach a conclusion. At the very least, he must go to Abdale. His word. To sneak off back to Edinburgh, to dismiss Fiona Burnett based on some scarcely believable accusations. That was not the kind of man he thought himself. 'Yes. I wish to see with my own eyes.'

2

THE THREE MEN TRAVELLED IN THEIR coach, Trent followed on behind. The rain had eased during the night and the temperature was climbing. Samuel thought it would be simpler to remove the wheels and sail her down the loch.

'What is all that?' Reid said as they mounted, pointing at the crates tied to the back and roof of the coach.

'Samples.' Eschewing his usual place beside Samuel, he enclosed himself behind the doors of the coach and retreated into his thoughts.

Over the last month on the islands he had been distracted. He had done his work diligently enough and amassed a collection of fascinating samples, but he could never quite focus his entire mind on what lay before him. Whenever he relaxed control of his attention, it returned to that beautiful, troubled girl sitting on the stone of Silma Hill asking him to take her away. What was he to do?

The coach stopped and he felt Samuel climb down, the jolt bringing him out of his reverie. He would just have to take things as they came. He got out and joined his fellow travellers on the jetty.

'Where's the ferry?' said Reid.

'It burned and sank,' said Trent. 'But there is still a rowing boat. You can see it tied to the jetty over there. We shall have to leave the coaches and horses here.'

Sir Robert grumbled something to his man. Trent rang the bell to get McBain's attention. It rang out clear across the water but there was no response. Trent scanned the shoreline, the village. He could see no one at all. He rang again.

'Where is everybody?' said Reid.

'A month ago this was a bustling village,' said Trent.

They waited, rang the bell periodically. Eventually McBain appeared. He stood regarding them for a moment before untying his boat.

Reid and Sir Robert went over first, the latter nearly pitching into the water trying to step from the jetty. Trent and Harrison waited. Trent took the opportunity to question Harrison more closely on their intentions.

'We are here to end this one way or the other,' he replied. 'Either sentences are carried out or all are pardoned.'

'Sir Robert can do that?'

Harrison looked at him, smiled. 'Sir Robert can do anything he likes in this area.'

Trent smiled back. 'What would be the best outcome, from Sir Robert's perspective?'

'Sir Robert would like nothing more than to be back in the capital as soon as possible.'

McBain picked them up and they joined Reid and Sir Robert in Abdale. The servants remained at the loch to organise things while Trent led them up the hill to the manse.

3

A GHOST TOWN, WINDOWS SHUTTERED, GARDENS overgrown. Chickens pecked at the roads, scattering at footsteps. Trent had walked through abandoned crofting communities on the islands, stone cottages collapsing in on themselves, nature reclaiming. Abdale had the same feel. When hope had been sucked out of a community, its absence hung like cobwebs on everything. He hammered on the door of the manse, peered through the study window. The room looked like a battlefield, destruction in every corner. He exchanged a glance with Reid. They checked the kirk next. It was here, sitting on the front pew, head in hands, that they found Burnett. He heard their footsteps but didn't look round, didn't look up. He was so tired, so very empty, he just wanted to be left alone, but still they came.

'Another?' he said. 'Who is it this time?'

'Another what?' said Reid.

His deep voice, unexpected and booming in the kirk, shocked Burnett to his feet. He stared at the four men before him like they were unearthly visitations. Trent was astonished by his appearance. His hair stood at scarecrow-like angles, his eyes were black, the skin underneath sagging with lack of sleep. His hands shook. 'Who? What? How are you here?' he finally got out.

'We're here,' said Reid, 'to find out what is going on in your parish.'

'I—' Burnett didn't know where to begin, what to say.

'Where are they?' Sir Robert demanded. Burnett had encountered him briefly on a visit to the capital and knew to be frightened of his power.

'The Tollbooth.'

'Dawkins?'

'Same.'

'Show us.'

Burnett scarpered by them, they followed. Harrison looked at Trent questioningly. Trent knew the meaning of it: 'Is this normal?' He shook his head.

Invaders marching through a conquered town, refugees fled, hiding. 'Where are the villagers?' Trent asked Burnett.

'Hiding. Or in the Tollbooth.'

'Hiding?'

'Lest they too end up in the Tollbooth.'

'What's that smell?' asked Harrison.

Burnett stopped walking, sniffed, like he had never noticed the smell before. 'Crops.'

'Crops?' said Trent. 'You mean the harvest?'

'It never happened.'

Near the Tollbooth a new smell replaced that of rotting crops: the stench of prisoners. Trent, Reid and Harrison reached a point where they could continue no further, the odour overpowering. Sir Robert looked at them with disgust and marched into the Tollbooth, returning moments later with Dawkins and Jimmy Ross, mounds of paper in their arms, terrified countenances. Sir Robert had not informed them of his intention to visit.

'There's an inn?' Reid said to Burnett.

'What?' said Burnett, distracted by the sight of Dawkins filled with fear. The two enemies stared hard at each other, but Sir Robert's presence shut Dawkins' mouth firmly.

'Yes,' said Burnett, eventually. 'This way.'

He took them to MacFarlane's and banged on the doors

and windows until Tam MacFarlane appeared. The sight of Dawkins and Burnett iced him. Sir Robert pushed him aside, pulled two tables together and ordered Dawkins and Ross to organise the papers upon them. Meantime Reid took control of their locale, instructing Mr MacFarlane and his wife to light the fire, to get food cooking and to bring wine.

Sir Robert, Harrison, Dawkins and Ross laboriously went through every stage of the investigation. Trent lacked the training and the authority to assist. He had come – it seemed mad to even think it. He had come to decide whether to marry. A marriage, at this time? In this place? He sat and listened to Reid question Burnett.

'You followed Kirk law exactly?'

'Yes. They brought me to the accused. I interrogated—' He shuddered as he said the words and Trent once again was drawn to the shaking in his hands.

'They all confessed?'

'Of course.'

'And signed?'

'They made their mark.'

'All?' said Trent, his voice far from under control. Burnett looked at him. Nodded. Trent wanted to go back to the Tollbooth, to see for himself, to get her out. He forced himself to stay in his seat. 'What will happen?' he asked Reid.

'If everything is in order,' he gestured at the four men and the piles of paper, 'they burn. If Sir Robert finds inconsistencies, mistakes or signs of anything untoward, they don't.'

'They go free?'

'We shall see. Oh,' he said suddenly, turning to Burnett, 'I have a letter for you.' Burnett eyed the proffered envelope with distrust. Everything new brought greater trouble. 'Don't worry,' said Reid, 'it is good news.'

The Minister took it and tentatively opened it as Reid watched, a benevolent smile that disappeared the second

Burnett let out a cry of rage and dropped the letter.

'What does it say,' asked Trent. Burnett offered it to him. Trent read aloud. 'Dear Reverend Burnett, regarding the recent submission of your paper entitled *Of A Pagan Idol Found At Abdale Peat-Moss*, the Historical Antiquities Society would like to extend to you an invitation to present this paper before the Society at a time to be decided.'

'This is good news, surely?' said Reid.

'He has the idol,' Burnett said savagely, pointing at Dawkins. 'Won't give it back.'

'It is evidence,' said Dawkins.

Reid looked at Sir Robert, who nodded. 'Evidence is not needed when a confession exists. Once the sentences have been carried out or the prisoners freed, Dawkins will return the idol to you.'

Trent shivered, chilled by Burnett's grin.

4

TRENT SLEPT UNSOUNDLY THAT NIGHT AND rose as soon as dawn showed the first hints of breaking. He came downstairs expecting to find the inn empty. They were the only guests and the MacFarlanes were far from being gracious hosts, keeping to their own rooms and giving the servants free run of the kitchens. He discovered Sir Robert, Harrison, Dawkins, Burnett and Reid still sat around the table of papers, blinking painfully when Trent opened the shutters and let morning in. He sent Samuel to make breakfast.

'Have you found something?' he asked the room.

'No,' said Harrison. 'Sheriff Dawkins and Reverend Burnett have followed the law and procedure exactly.'

'So nine people will burn.'

'Twelve now.'

Trent sat heavily, his appetite gone.

'I must sleep,' said Reid. He, Sir Robert and Harrison all took to their beds. Burnett drifted off like a ghost. Dawkins took his hat and went to the door. As he opened it, he turned back to Trent.

'She's going to burn, you know that, don't you?' Trent watched him but said nothing. 'You would be better served by returning home, Mister Trent. We have to be here. You do not. And nothing good is going to come from this. None of us will escape unscathed.'

5

WHILE THE OTHERS SLEPT TRENT FOUND Samuel and ordered him to prepare everything for an imminent departure.

'We're leaving today, sir?'

'Probably not today, probably in the morning. I do not know. But I want to be able to leave at a moment's notice. Move everything to the coach then come back here and don't leave the inn. I want to know where you are at all times.'

'Yes, sir, but is everything all right?'

'They are going to burn them,' he took a few steps towards the Tollbooth, stopped, turned back. 'I have to do something.'

'Can you save them?'

'Perhaps I can save one. When you return, bring my tan satchel with you.'

'The tan satchel, sir? The one with the—'

'Yes, Samuel. Now go.'

The stench from the cells was overwhelming but Trent was in no mood for bodily weakness and his step did not falter for a second. He pushed open the door and found Ross asleep on his cot. He passed through the office to the cells. Twelve prisoners in two cells. Those with strength were crouched in a tiny square of space, the rest, too weak, lay, heads resting on their cell-mates. They were gaunt, filthy and emaciated. They'd had the bare minimum of fluid and sustenance, just enough to keep them from dying too early. Split into cells by gender, Trent went to the female cell and looked for her. There at the back, upright but propped against the wall. She had been there longer than all but Eilidh, so the marks of torture had begun to fade, but she had been starved longer than all but Eilidh. Trent had no idea which one Eilidh was but guessed it was the weakest, most corpse-like one lying face to the wall. Fiona was staring vacantly into space. He said her name a few times but she didn't respond. One older woman gently stroking the hair of a girl lying in her lap turned her head to him. 'She is out of touch. Most of them are. Girls their age, to experience this.'

'Can she hear me?' The woman leant over and gently touched Fiona's face. She woke from her trance with a start, looked about her panicked. 'Fiona,' said Trent again. 'Can you hear me?'

A man. A new man. This wasn't one of the pain-giving ones. This wasn't one of the prisoners either. A face she knew. A memory.

'Fiona, can you speak?'

Speak? Talk? Words made bad things happen. Names. Speaking names changed things. She had said a name and now he was here.

She shook her head.

'I remember you,' said a male voice. Trent looked at the other cell. Through the dirt and injuries he recognised Murdoch Sangster, the young man he had seen on Silma Hill a month before. 'What do you want with Fiona? More questions?'

'I have some questions, yes.'

'Her father had some questions. Do you know what he did to her? To all of us.' He banged pathetically against the bars.

'I won't hurt her. You say you remember me. Do you know why I came to Abdale a month ago?'

Murdoch nodded. 'You were to marry her. Why are you back? You want a witch for a wife?' He laughed, hard and cold.

'Is she a witch?'

'As much as I am.'

'Are you?'

'It's not witchcraft set loose in Abdale, it's madness. Look around you. What is this if not the dream of a lunatic?'

'What were you both doing on Silma Hill that day?'

'Arguing. I loved her. I love her. Before all this started we loved each other. We wanted a future. We knew her father would stop us, but,' he laughed again. 'I never thought it would be like this.'

'You argued. Did you do… anything else?'

'She is pure still, if that's all that concerns you. I never did nothing like that. Although maybe I should have. Wouldn't have made me any more guilty in their eyes. I am going to burn anyway, maybe I should have spread some seed while I had the chance.' Like a clockwork mechanism winding down, the fight left him. He sagged against the bars. 'Can you do anything for us? Can you help me? Can you help her?' His voice had changed, the hardness gone. Trent wanted to say something. Give him some hope. Help him. He shook his head. Fiona was still looking at him. Had she heard what he and Murdoch had said to each other? He needed to think and he couldn't think in there. He shook his head again.

'Goodbye.'

'Henry,' she said, a croaking, rasping voice. 'Henry.'

He turned back, grasped the bars. 'Yes?'

'Henry. Help us,' she managed to get out before a fit took her. He looked at her, deep in her eyes. The cell, at the floor, the bars, the walls and barred windows. He made a decision.

He left. Ross was still asleep.

6

HE RETURNED TO THE INN WHERE Samuel was waiting for him. They went up to their room, empty now that Samuel had packed everything back onto the coach. 'Samuel, I am about to give you the opportunity to leave my service.'

'Leave, sir, but why? Are you not happy with my work?'

'Very. But I plan to do something that, if it goes awry, could have serious consequences. Frankly, I plan to break the law.'

'Is that all, sir? What makes you think I have never viewed the law as a substance with elastic properties?'

Trent laughed, some of the tension escaping. He expounded his plan to Samuel who rolled his eyes, frowned, even laughed once. When he had finished, Trent said 'I knew you would not like it. But I must do this. That is why I am giving you the option of leaving.'

'Sir, you mistake my dislike of the plan. It is not for moral reasons that I object, it is because the scheme is so manifestly bad.'

'But there is no other way.'

'Of course there is. There is always another way. If you would permit me –' Samuel took Trent's plan to pieces and put it back together again with a number adjustments.

'No, Samuel, I cannot ask you to do that.'

'You are not asking me, sir. I am volunteering. Besides, credit me with some moral feeling. There is not a single thing about this situation that I like. If there is something I can do, then I will. The fact that it also serves your wishes only makes it all the more desirable.'

'But you shall be taking all the risks. I cannot allow that.'

'Not really, sir. I will be doing all the work, but then is that not the arrangement between us?' he laughed. 'But the risk will all still be with you. Your relationship with one of the prisoners is well known. Blame will naturally fall on you. If it fails, you will be held responsible. This, obviously, is why I must do the work. You must at all times be with Reverend Reid and Sir Robert. Only an alibi of that strength can save you.'

'And you?'

'As long as you are safe, so am I.'

'Well, Samuel, it is a better plan. What do you need me to do?'

'Give me back your satchel, then when we go downstairs order me, in front of everyone, to go to the coach, prepare it for departure and to stay there all night to guard your possessions. Then until tomorrow morning make sure you are always with at least one of those men whose word will always be trusted.'

'Very well then, let's go.'

7

SAMUEL ROSE ON A WAVE AS his feet hit the path to the jetty. Speeding thoughts and rhythmic steps moving him forwards, he felt again that thrill of the game. The plan was straightforward enough and, like all plans, could only be undermined by two things: luck and the agency of others. Despite the scientific canals his thoughts travelled down and the chains of logic Trent had handed him, that small street boy still believed in luck. Some people are just lucky. Samuel was, but he knew luck alone was never enough.

Once clear of Angus Grant's barn he pulled up. Along the shoreline stretching west towards the ocean pyres were being built. Samuel shivered. He had seen executions before and the images had never left him. He hoped the three of them would be long gone before a spark was made. He reached the jetty but instead of calling McBain, he stepped down onto the sand and made his way to the ferryman's house. Boots up on a wood-burning stove, expired tobacco pipe bumping between sleeping teeth, McBain was passing the afternoon in his traditional fashion. On the sand next to his porch stood a pile of driftwood, a chopping block and an axe. Samuel hefted the axe and set to work.

At the first thunk, McBain woke with a start, his pipe dropping, emptying its remains down his shirt. 'What are you after there, lad?'

'Sorry to wake you, sir. I saw the pile and, as I'm at a loose end until my master needs me, I thought I'd lend a hand. You don't mind, do you?'

It would be an odd thing for McBain to mind someone chopping wood for him, but the unnaturally fast shift from dreams to reality had unsettled him. He eyed Samuel suspiciously, resumed his seat.

'I admire your home,' said Samuel, lining up the next piece. 'On the shore, facing away from the village. You can be alone if you want, be with company should the mood grab you.' McBain looked around him. Kept his silence. 'I'd love a spot like this, myself,' Samuel continued. 'I grew up in the city, all that smoke and brick. Aye, this is a peaceful spot right enough.' McBain snorted. 'You disagree?' Samuel asked him, casual as he could, bringing the axe through a wet branch.

McBain considered. Decided to speak. 'Peaceful? Not of late, lad. You call that madhouse peaceful?'

'Well, it's certainly quieter than Edinburgh. Surely this… situation is recent though. I heard it was just since summer.'

'Aye. Always some trouble round here, mind, but this is the worst I can think of. Folks always has problems with other folks but the things going on now, the things the Minister has done to those kids. Not right it is. Not right at all. Specially for a man of God. Over the seas you expect that kind of thing, but not here. Not at home.'

Samuel had everything into logs and kindling, began stacking them under the eves.

'Well,' said Samuel, gesturing along the shoreline, 'it'll all be over soon.'

'Aye.' He spat into the sand. 'All over. Twelve dead, youngsters among them. Mad.'

'If they're guilty—' began Samuel.

'Guilty? Guilty of what? Some queer things going on right enough but if Mary Dalziel and Fiona Burnett and all of them are witches then I'm a bullock's arsehole.'

'But the law?' Samuel stacked, trying to make his prompts sound casual, unplanned.

'What law? Only one law and that's God's law, and no God I ever prayed to burns wee lasses.'

'I wish there was something we could do to help them.'

'Aye,' said McBain, shaking his head. 'But the likes of us is powerless. With the Minister and Dawkins and that lot of titles you turned up with, things is too far gone.'

Samuel looked again at the pyres. 'I hope you're wrong,' he said. 'I've never been a big one for the law. Seems to me right and wrong are easy enough to see without a library of volumes.'

McBain nodded his head, spat again.

'All done,' said Samuel. 'Would you mind taking me across? We're leaving at first light and I need to get everything ready.'

He watched McBain row back. It would be risky. Once the old man had tied up the ferry and returned to his house, Samuel unloaded the biggest box from on top of the coach and cracked it open. Collecting these samples had been such hard work, and involved no small amount of danger as they scaled cliffs and outcrops. Seabird shit under his fingernails and his boots never dry. He shifted the case to the jetty and tipped the rocks into the loch, watching them settle out along the bottom. Everything was ready. Now he had to wait and pray his luck held.

8

SAMUEL HAD A THREE DIMENSIONAL PLAN of the village in his head. After the streets, wynds and closes of Edinburgh, Abdale was far from a challenge. Skirting the manse, keeping to the shadows, he ran, crouched low along the burn road, left hand holding Trent's satchel firm.

The village was still. People locked inside their homes, fearful, scared of demons, scared of their imagination, scared of their fellow man. No one would risk being seen outside at night, even for a full bladder. Samuel made it to the back of the Tollbooth without being seen.

A couple of inches above head height the open, barred window. Two cells. The window half in one, half in the other. The bisecting bars meeting it. This amount of powder, *p*, on this spot, fuse of *n* length, equalling *t* seconds. Done. Science, exact, precise.

Samuel hissed. Nothing. He hooted like an owl. Nothing. He looked around for something to stand on, something to get his head up to the window. Nothing. He whistled.

A head. Samuel recognised the face, gaunt and scarred though it was.

'I know you,' the head said.

'And I you.'

'You're with that man.'

'Trent. Yes. I'm here to help.'

Murdoch laughed, cold. 'Help? How?'

'Jailbreak.'

'Nonsense.'

'Look, we don't have time for a chat. I need you to get everyone away from the wall.'

'Why?'

'Because I'm going to blow it up. If they're near the wall, they'll die. Got it?'

Murdoch stared hard at Samuel, but he had nothing to lose. He dropped from sight, reappeared. 'Okay. Now?'

'Now get back and get ready to run.' He lit the fuse and ran back to the safety and darkness of the burn road.

Fire and stone, hell ripped through Abdale.

He had seconds. The calculations had been perfect. A hole big enough to pass through in the wall, Murdoch already helping people through.

'Where is she?' Samuel asked him.

'Fiona? You're taking her.'

'Yes.'

'Away from here?'

'Yes.'

'Good.' He dived into the other cell, returned with Fiona in his arms. She was out cold. Murdoch kissed her on the forehead, handed her gently to Samuel. 'Get her out. Make sure she's safe.'

'I will. You should run.'

'Where?'

Running in the dark. Fiona in his arms, the satchel swinging wildly.

The back of the manse, the foot of Silma Hill, she moaned.

Shouts, footsteps. The search was on. He had moments.

He needed luck.

He needed help.

This moment would decide everything. His original plan had been for them to swim across but that was out of the question.

Fiona could hardly walk, so weak and battered was her body. The cold, the current, the shock, any of it could kill her. He needed to get her across and into the case as fast as he could.

McBain was up, the noise of the village distinct in the night air. 'What's going on?'

'This,' said Samuel. He raised Fiona's limp head. 'We're getting her out of here.'

McBain looked at the torches dancing between buildings and trees, the shouts in the night. 'Where are you taking her?'

'Edinburgh. My master was to marry her before all this. We have no wish to see her burn. Do you?' Fiona groaned, Samuel shifted her weight. 'Come on, man. Take us across. You want to see her burn in the morning?'

McBain untied the boat and helped Samuel lower her in. He rowed slowly, Samuel urging him on, but he knew what he was doing. Hard rowing, splashing, fast movement would attract attention. They reached the jetty and got her onto dry land.

'Thank you,' said Samuel. 'You have saved us both.'

'Aye, well, you do well by her. I've done this for her, not you or your master.'

'You had better get back over,' said Samuel. 'If they see the boat gone, we are lost.'

'Don't you worry about me, just give your attention to her. I can take care of myself.'

'You're a good man.'

'Aye, well, that's worth damn all these days.' He pushed off, sliding into the darkness on the loch.

9

TRENT DID AS SAMUEL INSTRUCTED AND spent the day at the inn with the other men. Since Sir Robert was present in Abdale, the paperwork could be completed immediately and the sentences carried out. At eight o'clock all twelve witches would be burned. No space in the village big enough for such an event existed so it was decided that the loch shore would be the best place. Dawkins was given orders to prepare the fires and left to pressgang workers to the task. It was Sir Robert's intention to leave Abdale as soon as preparations were complete but by the time everything was arranged and a long, hearty lunch had been eaten, it was decided they should leave early in the morning. No man wanted to be there after eight.

'I shall be glad to see Abdale from the other side of the loch,' Trent said to Reid.

'I thought you came here to get married.'

'I came to give my apologies. It is a shame the way things have worked out, but I had already decided not to marry Miss Burnett.'

'That may be for the best.'

'I am sure none of this is for the best, sir, but I can see your point.'

Work done for the day, they settled in for an evening of cards and wine. The snow held off but the winds were bitter, and each man thought fondly of a warm bed. Trent worried what would happen if both Reid and Sir Robert retired early, so he endeavoured to make the evening an enjoyable one. He regaled them with anecdotes about his travels and his time with Dr Moore. When that grew tiresome he questioned Sir Robert on some of the more famous cases he'd been involved in over the years. As the night unfurled Trent became increasingly panicked. Perhaps Samuel had failed. Perhaps he had been caught. Perhaps. Perhaps. Perhaps.

Finally, just as Reid was signalling to his man, a monstrous clap echoed through Abdale. It had started.

'What was that?' said Reid.

'Thunder?' said Trent.

'It sounded like musket fire,' said Harrison.

The door burst open and Dawkins rushed in, clearly just out of his bed. 'You had better come quick, there has been a break out.'

They rushed through the dark streets to the Tollbooth where Jimmy Ross was in a panic. A hole had been blown in the back of the Tollbooth opening directly into both cells and most of the prisoners had escaped.

'Ross,' said Dawkins, 'how many are missing?'

'Eight,' he replied in a high pitched shout. 'Eilidh Sangster, Mary Dalziel, her mother and old Missus Sangster are still here.'

'The ones who cannot move in other words,' said Dawkins. 'They cannot have got far. They are all weak and they have only had a few minutes' start.'

They lit torches and split up. Trent made sure he stayed with Reid, down the burn road peering into the darkness.

'There's one,' said Reid, and they snatched hold of a man hobbling across the field and escorted him back to the Tollbooth. Ross had caught another and was now standing guard lest they escape again. Dawkins had dragged villagers out of their beds and the streets were torchlit. Trent followed Reid everywhere, making sure he was always either seen or heard.

It didn't take long before seven of the eight had been

rounded up. The only one still missing was Fiona Burnett. Trent couldn't quite meet Reid's eye. Dawkins surveyed the assembled villagers and visitors. 'Where's the Minister?'

10

LEAVING ROSS AND HIS RIFLE TO guard the prisoners properly this time, they raced over to the manse and burst through the locked front door. Burnett sat in his study, an empty bottle of wine before him, the letter from the Society shredded on the desk. He looked up, startled.

'Where is she!' Dawkins rushed behind the desk, lifted him by the scruff. 'I have got you now Burnett, tell us where she is.' Behind them villagers ran through the house searching.

'What is this? Reverend Reid, what is going on here? What is the meaning of this?'

'Dawkins, put him down. Burnett, can you account for your movements this evening?'

'My movements? I left you gentlemen at the inn and came home to prepare for tomorrow. I have been here ever since. What is going on?'

'Someone helped the prisoners escape from the Tollbooth. They've all been recaught. All except one.'

'Fiona? But—'

'No sign, sir,' said a voice from the hallway.

'Where is she?' said Dawkins. 'Where have you hidden her?'

'I have nothing to do with this. I have no knowledge of her whereabouts.'

'Liar. You heard the sentences were to be carried out and you helped her escape. You are the only one who would save her and none of the others.'

'It does look bad, Edward,' Reid said kindly, 'but if you

truly are innocent, then there is nothing to fear.'

Burnett drained. He knew exactly how much truth those words revealed. He had used them often enough.

'Keep searching,' said Dawkins. 'I am taking this one back and locking him up myself.'

From the back Trent watched. As Burnett was escorted out, Reid took Trent to one side, pointed a thick finger in his face. 'Dawkins was wrong. There are two people here who would seek to save Fiona Burnett. I am asking you now, once, did you have anything to do with this?'

'Reverend!' he said, 'how can you think such a thing. I have been with you all day and night.'

'Where is your boy?'

'He is with the coach guarding my possessions. You heard me order him there myself.'

'Yes, I did.'

Sir Robert had walked over and was listening. 'Convenient,' he said. 'Show me.' Trent started to complain, to argue, but Reid silenced him with a look. Harrison following on, they went down to the loch. Stretching along the shoreline from the jetty out beyond Tiki Rock stood twelve pyres waiting for the condemned. Trent kept his sight forward.

'I've a mind to retire and move,' said McBain, coming over. 'This village is a madhouse. A man can't get a decent night's sleep. Why people would want to cross at this hour I'll never understand. Come on then, get in,' he said.

'Ferryman,' said Reid. 'Has anyone else crossed tonight?'

'No, no one.'

'What about a young boy, about seventeen years old?'

'Well-dressed chap? I dropped him on the far shore this afternoon.'

'Has he come back?'

'No.' Trent fought to keep his face impassive. He looked at Reid who looked at Sir Robert.

'We had better check.'

Reid never took his eyes off Trent the whole time they crossed. Trent couldn't let a particle of his tension show. 'Samuel,' he called as he stepped onto the jetty. Please be here. 'Samuel, wake up.'

The coach rocked side to side and the door finally opened. A bleary-eyed Samuel looked out. 'Sir? Is everything all right? I thought we were leaving in the morning. I am sorry I was sleeping, sir. I will get ready to leave.'

Reid looked in the coach, circled it. Nothing.

'Sir?' said Samuel.

'There has been an escape from the Tollbooth. We were suspected but I trust that suspicion has been laid to rest?'

'Had to be sure,' said Reid. 'And now we are. Come, back to Burnett.'

'Samuel, you remain here. We are still leaving in the morning. I have no desire to see a burning.'

'Yes, sir.' Samuel watched them get in the boat and row away, his grin unseen in the dark.

11

FIONA WASN'T FOUND THAT NIGHT. BURNETT was questioned but he gave them no information and continued his denials. In the morning, the eleven remaining prisoners were taken down to the loch. Each in turn was tied to the stake in the middle of their pyre and given a chance to once more confess and ask forgiveness of God. In front of openly weeping villagers all besides Eilidh, Mary and old Mrs Sangster did so. These three said nothing, merely stared out over the loch, empty.

On the far side old McBain sat in the boat waiting.

Behind him, Trent and Reid. Reid had come in the boat, so he said, to say farewell, but both knew it was to check there were no extra passengers. 'You won't wait and travel with us?'

'Do you know how long that could be in coming?'

Reid shook his head. Now one condemned prisoner was missing and the Parish Minister was the chief suspect, his continued presence in Abdale was demanded.

'Besides,' said Trent gesturing at the pyres. 'I have no wish to see that.'

'As you wish.' Trent turned to climb into the coach. 'Henry,' said Reid. He turned back. 'I am sorry for asking, but considering what is ahead of me, I would be remiss not to. Fiona Burnett. You have nothing to do with her escape?'

'I know you are doing your job,' he said, putting a hand on the older man's shoulder. 'But no, I had nothing to do with it.'

'I just cannot believe it was Burnett. Aside from the fact that he has always put rules before anything else – this is the man who extracted the confession by which she was condemned in the first place – aside from that, how would he go about it? That explosion was perfectly calculated to break the wall but not injure those inside. Burnett fancies himself a scientist but really he is a keen incompetent.'

'Desperation can push a man to do anything,' said Trent. 'Both destructive and creative. Guilt is a powerful motivator, Reverend. I don't need to tell you that.'

'No,' said Reid. 'Well, take care, Trent. I am sorry you got caught up in all this. I feel responsible. It was, after all, me that arranged the match between you and the unfortunate Fiona.'

'Fret not, sir,' said Trent. 'A man proceeding with his eyes open cannot blame others if he trips.'

'I will see you back in Edinburgh soon.'

They shook hands. Reid watched the coach trundle off, then got back into the boat. As he crossed Loch Abdale the first pyre was lit. If Burnett was guilty, then Fiona would still be somewhere in Abdale. If Burnett was guilty, it was Reid's job to find out the truth. As the screams reached him he hoped Burnett wouldn't remain so stubborn. It had been many long years since he had conducted an interrogation.

On the shore the flames jumped high, fingers reaching around Silma Hill.

Acknowledgements

Lasting gratitude to Adrian Searle, Robbie Guillory and all at Freight Books; my agent, Judy Moir; my editor, Rodge Glass; Simon Sylvester, Robert Porter and Michael Callaghan.

For inspiration, Jeff Sanders and the National Museum of Scotland.

For everything, always, Patricia Inglis, Michael Maloney and Sarah Maloney.

With all my love, Minori.

Sources:

Of An Ancient Image, Found In November Last At Ballachulish Peat-Moss by Sir Robert Christison.

All Biblical Quotes from the King James Version.